KADE'S MATE

West Ridge Bears - Book One

K. C. WOODS

Published by Blushing Books
An Imprint of
ABCD Graphics and Design, Inc.
A Virginia Corporation
977 Seminole Trail #233
Charlottesville, VA 22901

K. C. Woods
Kade's Mate

Print ISBN: 978-1-64563-641-0
v2

Cover Art by ABCD Graphics & Design

To my husband who inspires my naughty imagination.

To my mom who has always supported me and worried about me. I love you, Mom. Don't read this one - it's way too dirty for you!

Prologue

March 13th
Kade

"Remind me again why I'm here," I asked my brother as we walked through the aisles of merchants at the annual home and garden show in Ridgewood. It wasn't that I didn't know, and it wasn't that I didn't appreciate the business side of it. It was just that, out of the two of us, Kain was by far more social and I had a strange sense of unease I couldn't figure out. Kit, my bear, was anxious and pacing inside me. I rubbed my chest to calm him.

"Networking, Kade," Kain reminded me with an eye roll. "Supporting the three businesses we invested in that are here today, getting out of the office and stretching our legs, and checking out the scenery." His eyes followed the backside of a curvy little brunette when he said that last part.

I elbowed him before anyone else caught him leering like a

perv. He grunted but didn't even try to hide the shit-eating grin that split his face.

"Grow up," I advised. "We're not going to get far *networking* once someone starts a rumor that the Barrett Brothers are a pair of horny dogs."

"That would be horny bears, thank you very much," Kain announced, a little too loudly.

I didn't even respond, walking away from him instead. I knew he'd follow. I stopped at a vendor advertising a new solar technology. Kain wandered to the next booth, where some hot girl was sitting in a hot tub. The entire Ridgewood Civic Center was blocked off for this event, the floor covered with different booths advertising popular or up-and-coming businesses from the area. There were four rows from what I could tell. We were halfway through the first row and I was getting more uneasy with every step.

I listened to the sales pitch for about thirty seconds, snagged a business card because it really was worth doing some further research, and then grabbed Kain's elbow and led him away from the area. The last thing he needed was a casual hookup.

He took it in stride and immediately stopped at the next booth, a local gardening company that specialized in growing fruit trees for our climate and was even teaching a seminar in the main area the next day. I listened with half an ear while Kain chatted away merrily with the owner.

We stopped at every booth on the west side of the civic center over the next hour. I was pretty bored, to be honest, it wasn't my scene, but Kain visited with everyone, taking business cards and giving out some of his own. Kain had always been the social butterfly of the two of us. The man could make friends anywhere.

It wasn't until we stopped at a landscaping company that specialized in authentic looking turf that I started to get *really* uncomfortable. Kit began raging inside of me, and no amount of chest rubbing would settle him. What the hell?

I smelled the sweetest fragrance and sniffed the air to identify the aroma.

Mate! I felt the jolt of awareness at the same time he screamed inside my head.

Fuck no!

My whole body lit up like I'd grabbed a live wire, my cock achingly hard in my slacks as I searched around frantically for the source. I'm slightly ashamed to say, I ducked behind the giant Astro Turf sign as I scanned the crowds of people.

There were so many people bumping elbows to get better views of the booths, I'm not even sure how I knew it was her. But when I saw her, I knew.

She was pretty tall for a woman, especially in those fuck-me pumps she had on. Long, trim legs led up to a navy skirt and jacket that hid tantalizing curves. Her honey blonde hair was twisted and clipped somehow at the back of her head. She was absolutely beautiful, remarkably so. Big eyes, elegant nose, high cheekbones.

She was absolutely everything I *didn't* want in a woman.

Because she was my mate.

As soon as she moved away, I approached the man she was talking to. He gave me several dirty looks, but finally let me copy the information from the business card she'd given him.

Abby Bradley.

"What in the hell are you doing?" Kain asked, peering over my shoulder.

I hid the note card from him and gestured towards the exit. "Nothing. We're leaving."

"But we're only halfway done!" Kain protested.

"You can come back tomorrow without me," I reasoned as I walked away.

We'd driven together, but as soon as I dropped him off, I

picked up a bottle of Johnny Walker and drove straight home to drown my sorrows.

Kit was pissed, raging inside me for not talking to her, claiming her. I didn't care. There was no way in hell I was going there. I'd taken her information, but I was convinced that it was only so I could do everything possible to avoid her like the plague she potentially was.

Yes, that was harsh. And yes, I know I was being a dick, but you can't judge me until you've seen what I've seen and know how bad mates can fuck up a man's life. Then you'd understand why I never wanted a mate. Then you'd understand why I didn't want her.

The only problem with that was, now that I'd found her, I didn't know how to live without her. As far as I knew, it had never been done. Once a bear meets his mate, it's almost impossible to keep him away from her, and they rarely separate. The bear marks the mate to seal the bond, usually during sex, and then he's forever sealed to her.

But *she's* not sealed to *him*, and that's where things can go wrong.

Anyone who wasn't familiar with bear culture might ask, if you're so afraid of your mate, why not just find a nice girl and mark her instead. Unfortunately, it's not possible. The man could bite a woman a hundred times, and it still wouldn't work. The mark has to come from the bear, and the bear will only mark that one destined mate. There's no way to trick the rule, and there are no second chances.

Each of my thoughts sunk me further and further into depression, panic and anger as the whiskey bottle started to dwindle. I wasn't even aware of what day it was when the pounding started on the door of my penthouse apartment. There were only two people who security would let up without calling me first: my assistant, Holly, and Kain.

And only one of them could pound on my door so obnoxiously.

"Fuck off, Kain!" I yelled, not even bothering to haul my ass off the plush reclining chair in my stylish apartment.

"Open this fucking door!" he yelled back.

"No!" I might've been a bit childish at that point, but the truth is, I probably wouldn't have been able to walk to the door anyway.

"I'll break it down!" he called.

"Use your key, dumbass!" Sometimes I wondered about him.

After some swearing, Kain finally figured out which key was my spare and opened the door.

"What the fuck, Kade?" He barreled in and then paused, taking in the dirty clothes on the floor from Friday after the home and garden show, and me sitting in my boxers with a bottle in one hand and a glass in the other. "What am I looking at right now?"

"I believe it's called a nervous breakdown," I told him, slurring my words, and chasing them with a drink.

"Why?" he persisted, taking a seat on the couch across from me.

"I saw her," I said, scowling into my empty glass.

"Who?" He jumped up lightning quick and grabbed the whiskey bottle out of my hand before I could pour more into my glass.

"Give that back." I lunged for the bottle, but he dodged me easily and I went crashing down to the floor, sending my empty glass flying. It shattered against the wall next to my chair. "You motherfucker."

"I didn't do that!" Kain set the bottle down on a bookshelf and reached down to help me into an upright position. We tried to get me vertical, but it just wasn't happening.

"Leave me!" I barked. "Get me a new glass."

"You've had enough," Kain informed me.

"There's never enough," I growled, flashes of Abby appearing in my mind. No amount of whiskey would be enough to drown out the memory of how beautiful she is, or how my dick was hard as steel before I even saw her, or how badly I wanted to throw her over my shoulder and run away with her.

"Who did you see?" Kain asked, his voice softening as he knelt on the floor next to me. "Mom or your mate?"

"Mate," I snarled, both at the truth and at the mention of Mom.

"It's not the end of the world, Kade."

"It very well could be the end of me!" I tossed back. He knew damn well why I didn't want a mate. He knew as well as I how deep my fears ran.

"What are you going to do, then?" He ran his hand through his hair and glanced up at the whiskey bottle longingly. "You know you missed work today?"

"Fuck, is it Monday already?" I worked myself up to my knees, using the couch as leverage against the swaying and dizziness. We'd gone to the garden show Friday afternoon. "What happened to Sunday?"

"It's lost in that bottle." He smirked when I glared at him. "Don't worry about work. I handled your meetings."

"Thanks," I grumbled, pulling myself up onto the couch to sit when it was obvious my legs weren't going to work enough for me to stand. I leaned back into the cushion and threw my arm over my eyes. "Can you handle my mate too?"

Kain let out a noise that sounded like a cross between a scoff and a chuckle. "No, but I do have an idea for a plan."

"Great, what is it?" I sat up, lowering my arm and leaning forward to hear his thoughts. There were two of him, but I focused on the one that wasn't swirling around the other.

Kain sat in the chair across from me, elbows on his knees,

leaning toward me as he considered it. "I think one of the things that kept Dad going for so long was that he had us," he said thoughtfully.

I bristled at the reminder of our poor father. What that man suffered was incomprehensible. "What are you suggesting? I get her pregnant and take the cub?"

"Yeah," Kain shrugged, chewing on his bottom lip. "Cover the girl with your scent, fuck every orifice, knock her up good, and then move on. With your cub."

I scratched my jaw, noting the significant beard growth I'd developed in the last few days and winced. "Wouldn't that involve a custody battle?"

"Not if she puts the cub up for adoption." Kain grinned. "How old is she? What's her situation like?" At my blank look, he continued, "We could get Lisa into the clinic to bend her ear a bit."

It was a stupid idea, but it was the best I had. Maybe if I just fucked her once, to satisfy Kit… Maybe if I had my cub… Maybe I could get through this without going completely crazy. I was very interested in any plan that potentially led to me not losing my mind and killing myself.

That may seem dramatic to some, but that's exactly what happened to our dad, so I knew how very likely it was.

"I could test her out for you, if you want, make sure she's worth the effort," Kain goaded me as only little brothers could.

It worked too. I shot off the couch, finding a strength and stability I hadn't had moments before, and glowered down at him. "If you fucking touch her…"

Kain stood up, matching my height, and smiling wickedly. "There you are. I was worried ol' Johnny had won."

I snorted, attempted to turn away from him, lost my balance and went toppling onto the couch. My asshole brother laughed. I growled. "Not a fucking word."

Chapter 1

April 14th
Abby

"Jack and Coke." I slid onto the barstool, trying not to grimace when my jeans stuck to the seat, and gave a cursory glance around. This dump was perfect for my current mood.

There were only a handful of empty stools left at the bar, and all of them were ripped or had been repaired by duct tape. *Obviously the work of a professional.* I snorted, things couldn't be that bad if I could still amuse myself.

The middle-aged bartender gave me a look, but I ignored him, looking around the bar again to see what kind of place I'd wandered into. The weathered booths lining the walls were only half-full and the tables in the middle were empty. Some bikers were playing pool near the back, their women propped against the wall like trophies.

I sighed, turning back to the bar, and my mind returned to

my own problems. Two years of my life I wasted on that cheating, disgusting pig. I really should've known sooner, the signs were there. It took walking in on him with my best friend, Liam, bent over the kitchen table to truly open my eyes. They could both go to Hell. I was done with men.

The bartender put my drink in front of me and ran my debit card without comment. Perfect, I was not in the mood to chat.

"Here alone?" A guy plopped onto the stool next to me.

Giving him a brief glance out of the corner of my eye, I noted he was kind of cute and about my age. I had a strong urge to smack him, just for being male.

"Yes, and I prefer to keep it that way, if you don't mind." I raised my drink and dismissed him callously.

He didn't take the hint. "Bad day, huh?" He smiled at me sympathetically. "I've been there. After a few drinks, you'll forget all about it."

"I hate to be a bitch, but please leave me alone." I sighed.

Simon, my ex, used to tell me all the time that I could be a bitch. I just prefer to cut through the pretentious bullshit. Give it to me straight and honest, and I'll do the same.

I didn't get where I am today by pussyfooting around people. My success came from persistence, hard-work and a straightforward approach. I shouldn't have to apologize for that. With Simon, I constantly was.

Every time something reminds me of Simon, I realized just how unhappy I'd been. Life shouldn't be lived walking on eggshells. Love shouldn't be experienced with excuses and lies.

Was it ever really love? I had thought so. I'd been so awestruck by his charisma and potential in the beginning, I was blinded to his flaws. Namely, the fact that he was a philandering bisexual pig.

I downed the rest of my drink and motioned to the bartender for another.

Two months of wallowing in self-pity after our explosive breakup, and I'd finally realized that I could do so much better.

There was nothing wrong with me, unless you count my abrupt personality, which I didn't. I was smart, I owned my own company, I was pretty, five-eight and curvy, with long blonde hair and blue eyes. Some would say I was quite a catch, I thought.

I could definitely find someone who made me happier than Simon ever could. Not that I even needed a man to make me happy. I probably should just stay single for a while. I didn't know what I should do, and I hated feeling that way.

The bartender placed my drink in front of me. I gulped down half, wanting to drown out my doubts, my indecisiveness, my sadness.

"What do you do?" the guy, who was still sitting next to me, asked suddenly.

"What part of this are you not understanding?" I sneered, pissed that he wasn't taking the hint. "Go away."

"There's no reason to be rude," he replied. "I just wanted to talk."

"Leave," a deep voice growled behind us.

My whole body broke out with goosebumps, and I spun around to see what sort of man had caused such a visceral reaction.

I gawked up at the hulking stranger, he must be at least six-five with huge shoulders. His t-shirt strained against his thick biceps and wide muscular chest. Tattoos peeked out from the hem of his left sleeve. Faded jeans hugged his tree-trunk sized thighs, with an impressive bulge in front. *Holy mother of sex on a stick.*

I forced myself to look up at his face, as I heard the man next to me almost tip over the barstool as he scurried away.

The stranger's eyes almost looked like they were glowing,

bright green and yellow around the iris as he looked down at me, a cocky smirk on his full lips. He had a few days' worth of stubble on his angular jaw and wavy dark brown hair.

Heat flooded my cheeks as I realized how long I'd been silently gawking at him. I couldn't help it though, my heart was pounding wildly, my body tingled with an awareness I'd never felt before, my panties were instantly soaked.

"Hello, little girl." He perched on the barstool and faced me, pinning me with his intense eyes.

"I'm not interested," I forced through clenched teeth. Even with my intense physical reaction, I was still on the fence about letting a man into my life. It was probably better to err on the side of caution, right?

"Yes, you are," he challenged me, raising one eyebrow. "And you're going to come home with me."

"Why would I do that?" I scoffed at his presumption.

I'd only ever had sex with Simon, and I didn't consider myself the type of girl to be into one-night stands.

"Because we're going to fuck away whatever heartache you're attempting to drown." He grabbed my glass from my hand and drank the rest. Then he leaned towards me, dropping his voice, his breath tickling my neck. "I'll fuck you until you can't even remember his name. And the best part is, you won't even have to learn mine."

I gulped. When he put it like that, it didn't sound like a bad idea at all. Maybe it was exactly what I needed. My body was definitely on board, as I leaned towards him, breathing in the smell of pine trees and man.

"Then what am I going to scream when I'm coming?" I bit my lip nervously. Could I really do this? Could I be this girl, just for one night?

"Daddy." He grinned mischievously.

"How very kinky of you," I teased, raising one eyebrow in question. "Are you a daddy?"

"No, but I'll put you over my knee and spank you if you misbehave." His eyes raked down my body.

He slowly raised his arm, as if waiting for me to object, and then trailed a single, large finger down my bare arm. I shivered as electricity coursed up my arm and tightened my nipples. If one little touch could set my nerve endings on fire, I couldn't imagine what it would feel like to have him touch me somewhere more *private*.

"What will you call me?" I asked curiously, just for clarification.

"Whatever I want to." He took my arm suddenly and pulled me off the stool.

I allowed him to lead me out of the bar, but as soon as we stepped out into the cool night air, an uncertainty came over me. I yanked my arm back.

"I protest at being manhandled," I told him with all the indignation I could muster.

He responded by throwing me over his shoulder and slapping me on the ass. I yelped in surprise and kicked my legs.

Secretly, I was more turned on than I'd ever been. Being thrown around like a ragdoll was not something that had ever happened to me before, and apparently I liked it.

He put me down and helped me up into a new black Silverado. I took the moment alone to admire him as he walked around the hood of the pickup. He moved gracefully for a man of his size. He jumped into the pickup and pulled out of the parking lot.

I didn't even care that I was leaving my car there, I would've had to get a cab home anyways after drinking. I hadn't really thought that through when I'd pulled in randomly.

I'd been on my way home from our latest remodel project, and dreading another night of sitting alone watching reality

TV. When I saw the bar, I'd thought a stiff drink might be exactly what I needed.

I might have decided that getting Simon out of my life had been for the best, but I was still sad and painfully lonely. I hadn't only lost Simon, I'd lost my best friend too. When you had a fortitude for being blunt and worked with the single-minded focus that I did, friends were hard to come by.

I was lost in my thoughts, and not paying attention to where the stranger, albeit hot man was taking me, until he pulled into the downtown Marriott.

"Are you from out of town?" I asked as we stepped out of the pickup and walked into the elegant building.

"Good guess." He grinned at me, his eyes gleaming with humor. I felt like he had an inside joke that he wasn't sharing.

"Business or pleasure?" I didn't know why I was even asking him, it didn't matter if this was just going to be one night of fun.

How had I even gotten here? I was starting to get really nervous. I pulled at the bottom hem of my shirt anxiously as he pushed the button for the elevator.

"Bit of both, I hope." He chuckled. The elevator doors slid open and he guided me on with his hand at the small of my back.

After a quick ride, the elevator doors opened to his floor. We walked down the hallway to a room and he unlocked the door. As soon as we were shut inside, he turned to me. His eyes darkened visibly.

"Strip," he commanded.

I narrowed my eyes, even though my body tingled at his demanding tone. Was that seriously going to be how he started things? I'd never been in a situation like this before, but I'd imagined there would be kissing, groping, tearing at each other's clothes.

He crossed his arms over his chest and waited for me to

follow orders. A small smirk played at the corner of his mouth, and I got the sudden inkling that maybe he was hoping I'd disobey. He had offered to spank me, after all.

I wasn't sure how I felt about the spanking business, but I decided that I'd made it this far, and I wasn't the type to chicken out. I started undoing the buttons of my blouse slowly, giving him a little show.

Kicking off my shoes, I unzipped my jeans and pushed them down my legs. I turned away from him and slid my shirt off my shoulders, letting it fall. I unhooked my bra and dropped it. Then I pulled my panties down and kicked them away.

I was left in just my necklace, a single floating diamond I'd gotten from my parents when I turned eighteen, the last birthday present they'd ever given me. Apparently, women don't celebrate birthdays after they turn eighteen.

"Turn around." His voice was low and gravelly.

My nipples tightened even harder than they already were from the excitement and the air. I slowly turned around to face him, squaring my shoulders with a bravado I didn't quite feel.

He had removed his shirt, shoes and socks during my strip-tease and was standing in just faded jeans. His chest and shoulders were enormous, his muscles bulging further with each breath. A large tattoo covered his left shoulder, starting just above his elbow, in an intricate design featuring a willow tree and bears. His chest had a sprinkle of dark chest hair that travelled south to… I gulped at the size of the tent in his pants.

"Come here." His voice broke through the mini-panic I was having at the size of him.

Running on sheer reflexes, I stepped towards him until we were mere inches apart.

He took me by the upper arms and pulled me against him

roughly. I gasped at the sudden contact against his hard body, my skin burning everywhere it touched his.

"You are a dirty little girl, aren't you?" Dropping his face into the crook of my neck, he licked me and spoke against my skin. "You like when I push you around?"

Whimpering a reply, I tilted my head. He licked and sucked the spot just below my ear. I moaned and pressed against him harder.

I had no idea how he was making me feel this way, everywhere he touched felt like heaven. Every lick of his tongue sent tingles shooting through me. Every nip of his teeth had me gasping. Nothing I'd experienced with Simon could ever compare to this. The way my body responded to him, like it was made for him to command.

"Get that ass on the bed," he growled against my neck, as he slapped my ass hard. "On your back. Spread your legs."

I did as instructed, and he stood at the end of the bed and stared down at me. I squirmed under his scrutiny. I'd never been so turned on, and I wanted him desperately.

I'd forgotten all my fears and doubts, all I cared about was how he made me feel. For the first time in my life, I didn't care about anything other than the man in front of me and chasing the splendor of what I was feeling.

My stranger stalked toward me like a predator, slowly inching his way between my thighs. I buzzed with anticipation, my arousal running down my thighs.

I wanted to blush at how obviously turned on I was, it was on the tip of my tongue to apologize, but that wasn't me.

He lowered his head to my most intimate place and licked me from back to front in one single perfect stroke. I cried out, grasping his hair fiercely, my nails scraping against his scalp. He licked each side and then down the middle again. Stroking circles around my entrance and teasing around my clit, but never quite giving me what I needed. I squirmed in frustration, tightening my hold on his hair and trying to guide him where I needed him.

He pushed two large fingers into me, and I gasped. He licked around my clit as his fingers worked inside me. I was so close, I just needed a little more attention on my clit. I wiggled my hips, trying to get him to give me what I wanted. He refused to be rushed, as he pushed a third finger into me, stretching me, and driving me crazy.

I was a moaning and writhing mess, juices flowing out of me and coating his fingers.

"Come." His voice was guttural, and he finally pressed his tongue to my clit.

I screamed out in glory, instantly coming, clenching hard around his fingers. Delicious shivers traveled down my limbs, and I basked in it. My entire body shook and spasmed as white lights danced in front of my eyes. By far the best orgasm I'd had in… ever.

My body went limp, and I was faintly aware of him moving away and getting undressed. I thought I heard the sound of a condom, and then he was above me.

I didn't even manage to get a look at him, but when he lined himself up to my opening and started to push in, I knew I'd been correct in my assessment of his size. He wasn't just long, he was really thick. It stretched me as he continued at a slow and steady pace until he was buried deep.

"Fuck, you feel incredible." He lowered himself to his elbows, and I thought he was about to kiss me for the first time, but he dropped his head into the crook of my neck instead and moved experimentally. He groaned. "You're so fucking wet."

He started fucking me with a brutal ferocity, and I could barely manage to do anything but hold on. I wrapped my arms and legs around him as he pounded into me.

I'd never come without clitoral stimulation before, so

when my orgasm hit without warning, I was both surprised and delighted. He came with a grunt almost immediately after.

He pulled out suddenly, and I wasn't sure what to expect, but it definitely wasn't him kneeling next to my head and holding his cock near my face.

The size of it startled me. I'd had that thing inside of me? How was that even possible? I'd never seen a dick besides Simon's and that was laughable in comparison.

"Clean it off," he demanded.

I obeyed, hesitantly at first, but then I was sucking him deep into my mouth and marveling at how he was still hard after he came. Something was nagging me in the back of my mind, but I didn't focus on it as I licked and sucked our mutual cum off his cock.

He began moving his hips slowly, but soon was basically fucking my mouth and there was nothing to do but take it. He held my head firmly with his hands, grunted out a warning and then came down my throat. I swallowed quickly to avoid choking.

"Good girl," he mumbled, stroking my hair, as he waited for me to finish swallowing the last of his cum. It didn't even occur to me to be annoyed by that comment, I was too turned on by everything he did.

He pulled out of my mouth without warning and then moved down on the bed. He flipped me over like a rag doll and pulled my hips up. He thrust his still rock-hard cock inside me, and I cried out at the deep penetration.

He started pounding into me immediately, not allowing me to catch my breath. I felt moisture and then his finger at my back hole. He pushed one into me, and I screamed at the unexpected intrusion. He added a second finger and didn't let up. Instead of being ashamed, I was even more turned on at the feeling of being so full of him.

"Filthy fucking girl," he growled and fucked me harder. He worked in a third finger, stretching me.

I was seeing stars, and I knew I was going to come again, soon.

He reached up with his free hand and grabbed my hair, using it as a handle as he pulled and pushed and grunted. I was being used in the most disgusting way, and I loved it.

Nothing outside of this room mattered, not the past, not my work. Only he and I existed. Only our bodies, our sweat, our pleasure.

My orgasm came on slow but stronger than ever. I gripped the bedding for support. It burned inside me stronger and harder, and it was overwhelming in its brutality.

"Fuck! Daddy!" I screamed as I shook and trembled, trying to stay up on my knees as I came even harder than before.

He grunted and continued to push into me before he came too.

I collapsed and that nagging feeling returned. I was missing something, but I couldn't think straight to figure out what it was.

He licked the side of my neck and ran his hands down my back to my ass. He could not seriously still want more, could he?

My answer came a second later when he licked and kissed his way down my back.

"How?" I croaked.

"I'm not done with you," he growled and bit me on the ass. He spread my cheeks apart and licked around my back hole.

I heard something snap and then felt cold liquid on my ass. He could not possibly be thinking about putting his giant cock in my ass. It would split me apart.

"You're too big," I managed a weak protest.

He ignored it. He pulled my hips up and pushed my shoulders down. I thought about struggling and running away, but I was too sated. Let him use my body for tonight. It would heal. I was beyond caring.

I felt his fingers rub my clit and my body perked back to life instantly. Maybe I could have one more orgasm. I felt him slide a silicone toy into my pussy, and I groaned. Between his magical fingers on my clit and the dildo inside me, I was definitely good for one more. Then he shifted, and I felt his girth against my backside.

He pushed into the ring of muscle, and I cried out at the invasion. I'd let Simon back there a couple of times, at his insistence, but it wasn't my favorite thing.

My stranger's fingers continued to rub wicked circles on my clit, combined with the toy inside me, and his cock pressing against me, the sensation was overpowering. My arms shook, I didn't know what was coming, but I wondered if I'd survive it.

I felt him add more lube as he pushed in inch by fat, delicious inch. He paused, pulled out a little, added more lube and then pushed all the way in.

Oh, fuck. I was so full. Completely stuffed with him and the toy. He gave me a minute to adjust to him this time. His fingers stroked and circled my clit. He leaned forward and used his free hand to pinch and tease my nipples.

He pulled out slowly, and I gasped. He pushed in even slower, and I moaned. It was all so much, too much. I couldn't possibly survive this, but somehow I felt it would be worth it. He did it again, slow out and slower in, each time eliciting whimpering noises from me. He gradually began thrusting in earnest as the pain and pleasure warred within me.

His fingers worked skillfully on my clit and nipples, and then the pleasure started to overpower the pain. I was on sensation overload, and my vision was starting to blur as he fucked me.

I screamed and screamed as my orgasm shattered me. I couldn't think straight. I couldn't breathe. I couldn't see. I felt his teeth at my neck, and then he bit me... hard. Red hot pain tore through me.

"Mine," he growled in an animalistic and unnatural voice. Then he roared as he came, *"Abby."*

And I promptly passed out.

Chapter 2

April 15th
Abby

I had no idea what time I'd passed out or how long I'd been asleep, but it was afternoon by the time I woke up – alone – the following day. Housekeeping wasn't pounding on the door insisting I leave, though, so I didn't rush.

Every muscle in my body ached and spasmed as I rolled off the bed. My knees buckled, and I collapsed in a heap. I giggled as I pulled myself up and tried again. I'd heard guys brag about fucking a woman so thoroughly she'd walked funny the next day, but I'd obviously never experienced it before.

Abby. I heard his voice in my head, suddenly remembering the way my name had sounded on his tongue. How had he known my name? Did someone say it at the bar? No, nobody knew it. I knew I hadn't said it.

Maybe he caught a glimpse of my driver's license, that was

in my wallet, inside my purse. Unlikely. Had we met before? I was fairly sure I'd remember meeting a man of his dimensions and demeanor. I guess it didn't really matter, I'd never see him again.

I stumbled into the bathroom and gasped as I caught sight of myself in the mirror. Forget my extreme post-fuck bedhead, I had a huge hickey on my neck. It was bigger and darker than any I'd ever seen before. I could see the red teeth marks beneath the black and blue bruise.

I touched it tentatively, and winced at the sharp pain. What a brute! I couldn't believe he gave me a hickey! Of everything he did to me last night, this was the one thing that annoyed me the most.

I turned the shower on the hottest setting and stepped inside. I let the hot water soothe my sore muscles before washing my hair with the lavish hotel products. I lathered the soap and started washing my body.

When I scrubbed between my legs, I couldn't help but remember the feel of him there last night. He'd fucked me, then made me suck him off, then fucked me again, then fucked my ass! He was insatiable. Maybe he'd taken Viagra or something. *He must have stock in Trojan,* I mused with a chuckle.

Then, I froze. Trojan. Condoms.

I'd heard a condom wrapper the first time he'd fucked me, didn't I? I sucked him off right after and I didn't taste latex. I'd tasted his cum and… mine. *Oh fuck!*

I rinsed quickly and ran out of the shower and into the bedroom. Completely oblivious to the water I was dripping everywhere, I searched through the garbage and around the bed. No used condoms. No condom wrappers.

Fuck! How could I have been so stupid? So reckless? I quit taking the pill when I'd caught Simon fucking Liam and now… oh no, what if he had a disease? Forget getting knocked up by a stranger, what if I got AIDS?

My stomach revolted, and I ran back into the bathroom to throw up. What had I done? What the actual fuck had I done?

June 9th

Kade

"You told me to fuck her, I fucked her!" I yelled at Kain, who had unceremoniously barged into my office to give me his opinions. Again.

"I didn't tell you to fucking mark her!" he yelled back. "That was definitely not part of the plan."

I winced, one of his busybody spies must have told him, but I didn't let that stop me from my defensive retort. "Fuck every orifice, you said. Knock her up good, you said. What's done is done. It won't affect me. Just get over it. We'll get the kid and move on."

I shuffled some papers on my wide mahogany desk, pretending to establish order when I felt so out of control. I didn't want to look at my brother, standing in front of my desk, as we argued about my mate problem for the thousandth time.

"It won't affect you?" He choked on the words, hands waving wildly in the air. "You're never going to recover from this, Kade! It's bad enough that you're refusing to take your mate to your side, you chose to fuck her and knock her up against her knowledge, and then you marked her! Do you know what that means? You'll never be able to…"

"I know!" I cut him off. I couldn't stand to hear it said aloud. I knew exactly how bad I had fucked up. "I know, okay?

It just happened. It was really intense, beyond anything I'd ever felt before, and I lost control for a split second and fucked up."

"Are you sure you don't want to just take her?" His eyes flashed with sympathy as he plopped down onto one of the chairs across from my desk. "It would be so much easier."

"For whom?" I scoffed, picking up a random file and shuffling the papers.

"For you, jackass." He sneered at me.

"It'd be so easy after I kidnap her and she hates me forever," I replied sarcastically, tossing the file aside carelessly. "Pass. Next?"

"You're impossible." He rubbed his head, looking away from me. "Not every woman is like Mom."

"I'm not interested in doing the research," I snarled and narrowed my eyes. "Do you have anything work related to discuss, or are you just in here to bust my balls?"

"I have a bad feeling about this." He crossed his arms over his chest and glared at me.

I returned an identical glare, unwilling to back down.

I never wanted a mate and he knew it. Our mother had assured that Kain and I were both completely ruined on the idea of happily ever after.

As soon as I'd sobered up, I'd done a full background check on her, Abigail Rae Bradley. She was twenty-five, never married, no kids. She owned a small real estate company, buying and selling old houses. She also owned six investment properties and an old warehouse. Impressive for a young woman. She was very comfortable financially, but lived in a small, one bedroom apartment in a fairly shitty neighborhood and drove a ten-year-old Chevy Malibu.

Her dad was some kind of investment banker – obviously where she got her business ethic – and her mom was a high society wannabe, spending money she didn't have and never worked a day in her life. No brothers or sisters, and the only friend mentioned was a man.

"Are you even listening to me?" Kain snapped me out of my pondering of my mate.

"No," I answered honestly, picking up another random file and shuffling the contents.

"Stop daydreaming about her cunt for five minutes," he snapped. Kain was younger than me by ten months, but we were as close as twins. His eyes had more green and mine were more yellow, and he had a scar above his eyebrow, otherwise we were pretty much identical. He was my best friend, and the only person in the world who could speak to me like that and get away with it.

"I wasn't thinking about her cunt, asshole." I grabbed the nearest hard item, which happened to be a stapler and tossed it at his head.

He caught it easily with a smirk. Setting the stapler on the corner of the desk, out of my reach, he regarded me with a look that said he was waiting for me to continue.

"I was thinking about my kid," I lied, unwilling to admit that I'd simply been wondering about her.

"Ah yes." He nodded in approval at the change in topic. "She just had her first doctor appointment. She's not going to try to get an abortion so we won't have to deal with that. Lisa's going to approach her at the next one to discuss adoption, and see if she's compliant before we take more drastic measures."

"What's the backup plan?" I asked, suddenly realizing we hadn't discussed it. "If she doesn't willingly go for adoption."

"Greenhope," he answered automatically.

"You're kidding," I groaned. Greenhope was the name of the old, rundown family house I'd inherited. It was just on the outskirts of our community, close to the mountain range south of town, and would be a perfect place to raise a kid, if it wasn't currently such a shithole.

"Renovating old houses is her thing," he reminded me needlessly.

"Living in a bear community and raising a bear isn't her thing," I shot back.

"She won't have a problem in the community, not only did you cover her with your scent, you also marked her. Everyone would leave her alone." As he said it, I had an unexpected feeling of pleasure at knowing that no other bear would dare to touch what was mine.

"What else?" I pushed on, quelling my possessive nature.

"She'll have to be acclimated and adapt," he said without hesitation.

"Why do I feel like such an asshole?" I groaned and rubbed my chest, hoping to dull the ache that had formed after my night with her and only continued to get worse.

"Because you are." He shrugged nonchalantly. "The only other option is to kidnap the baby and raise it yourself."

"Let's just do that," I said without thinking, setting the file down and picking up another. "Leave her out of it. Let her remain naive to our world and continue on with her life."

"Now you're really being an asshole," he pointed out, running his hand through his hair in exasperation. "You think she'd just be able to happily go about her life if you kidnapped her baby?"

"Mom would have." My lip curled in disgust.

"She's not Mom!" he roared suddenly.

His outburst gave me pause. Mom was a special breed of bitch, never giving two shits about either one of us. I knew most women weren't like that, many of the moms I knew were actually loving and attentive. Maybe Abby would be like them. Her background check suggested otherwise, but just... maybe.

"Fine," I conceded hesitantly. "But I'm keeping it as a backup-backup plan."

"Of course you are," he sighed, then leveled me with a stern look. "In the meantime, it's off the table."

"Can we get back to work now?" I handed him the file on the new downtown project I was holding and put an end to this.

Chapter 3

July 7th
Abby

"I'll see you in four weeks for your next appointment then." Dr. Walsh smiled warmly at me as she stood. "Just wait here for one minute, Lisa will be in to speak with you."

The doctor walked out and not even a minute later, a well-dressed woman entered. She couldn't have been much older than me, maybe early thirties. She wasn't a nurse, and I hadn't seen her before. Her clothes suggested business-professional and didn't belong in a doctor's office. My sense of unease prickled instantly.

"My name is Lisa Adkins," she said politely as she entered and perched gracefully on the seat Dr. Walsh had just vacated. "I understand you're pregnant. How are you feeling about that? Do you have a support system?"

"Are you a psychologist or something?" I asked skeptically.

"More of a social worker." She smiled mildly. "I help with support groups, prenatal classes, new parenting classes and adoptions."

She put a slight emphasis on the final word, and I bristled, regarding her warily. "Adoptions?"

"Yes, of course." Her expression didn't change. "It's always an option. Especially for young ladies with no support system. Are you married?"

"No." I narrowed my eyes. I didn't like this. Something about it was rubbing me the wrong way. "But I'm not putting my baby up for adoption either."

"All right." She nodded once. "So, what are your plans? Do you have suitable housing? Do you have anyone else who will be there to support you? Parents? Friends?"

"Look, I'm sure you're just doing your job, but I'm not comfortable discussing this with you." I stood abruptly. "I'll be fine. I've always been self-sufficient."

I strode out of the office. I stopped at the front desk and calmly told them if Lisa was at my next appointment, I would be finding another doctor. Then I marched out, feeling out of sorts.

I still couldn't believe I'd been stupid enough to let the giant, dominating asshole get me pregnant. I'd almost cried with relief when the STD tests all came back negative. He was right though, when he was done with me, I didn't remember my ex's name. Not literally, of course, but I almost never thought about it anymore.

All I thought about was having a baby. It hadn't been on my five-year plan, but in my head, I would admit I was excited. Would I have a son who would grow into a six-and-a-half-foot giant with glowing green-yellow eyes? Would I have a daughter with my blonde hair and blue eyes?

I was almost three months along, and I was feeling good about having a child. I was fine with raising him/her alone.

Lots of women were single mothers, and I was stronger than most.

My own parents weren't the most desirable role models. My dad was an avid businessman and stretched his meetings as long as possible to delay coming home. I'd always suspected he had at least one mistress. My mom was more concerned about her image and her next facelift to care what he – or I – did.

I was basically raised by a nanny until I was nine, and my mom fired her for giving me cookies and milk after school one day. It wasn't something we did regularly, but a girl in school had told me that I had a stupid name, and I'd gone home crying.

Michelle let me have cookies and made me feel better, but I still don't let people call me Abigail. I didn't hear what Mom said to Michelle, but now that I'm old enough to reflect, it was probably something about not wanting a fat daughter.

I wouldn't be like my parents. I'd have to get a nanny for when I worked, but I could reduce my hours, and when I was home from work, I'd be present in my child's life. I'd be the one to get my daughter cookies and milk when she was sad. I'd be the one putting Band-Aids on scraped knees and drawing the evening bath. I could even teach a son how to throw a ball, if it's a boy. I was confident in my capabilities.

I drove home and entered my small apartment just west of downtown Ridgewood. I'd lived there since I'd moved out of my parents' house when I was eighteen years old. I had the money for a nicer place, but I just hadn't done it yet. When I was with Simon, I'd spend most nights at his place anyway.

Now I looked around the small rooms and realized it was time to start looking. I could move into one of the apartment buildings I owned, but I didn't really want to. I had three houses in different stages of renovation at the time, but none of them really fit my taste either. I'd have to start looking for something else.

As if on cue, my phone rang. I scrambled through my purse to find it.

"Abby Bradley," I answered professionally. "May I help you?"

"Good afternoon, Ms. Bradley," a deep voice answered. It reminded me so much of my mysterious giant, I shivered. "My name is Kain Barrett. I stumbled upon one of your renovations and was very impressed. I've looked at a few houses you've done. You have good taste."

"Thank you." I smiled at the praise. "Are you in real estate?"

"I own an investment firm, Bare Industries. It's a family business, and we really enjoy taking on new projects."

"What does that have to do with me?" I asked skeptically. My company is small, but it's profitable and I don't need help. I also don't want to expand or partner with a large company like Bare Industries. I'd heard of it, of course, everyone in town had seen their billboards and ads.

I'd heard the current owners had taken over their father's work and were really starting to make waves. They had their fingers in new businesses, urban planning, rural developments and even non-profit work in both Ridgewood and the neighboring suburban town of West Ridge. I hadn't crossed their paths yet, and I was fine with that.

"Nothing yet." His vague answer annoyed me. "I have an old house, Greenhope, just outside the city, in West Ridge. I'm looking at putting it on the market, and I'd like to give you the first chance at it."

"Why?" I continued with my skeptical train of thought. What did he really want from me?

"Well, to be frank, West Ridge is my home and there are several old, rundown houses that someone needs to take responsibility for." He sighed dramatically, but it sounded forced. "I'm really hoping to get you interested in the area and take some initiative to restore some of the eyesores."

"So, just to make sure we're clear, you're not going to try to buy out my business or anything like that?" I needed to get everything out in the open before I agreed to anything.

"Did you want me to?" he asked, sounding confused.

"No!" I snapped. "If you had tried, this conversation would already be over."

He remained quiet for a minute. "I admire your spunk. I'll have my assistant, Holly, send you the information, and our real estate agent can meet you at the house for a tour. Take a look and then decide. I promise I'll never try to buy your company or force you into the corporate conglomerate. Deal?"

"Sure, I'll take a look."

I disconnected and walked into my bedroom, scowling when I caught sight of myself in the mirror. No matter what I did, or how much makeup I caked on in the morning, that damn bite mark was still visible. The bruise was gone, but the teeth marks remained, and likely always would.

It wasn't bad enough that I'd be raising his baby, he'd left his mark on the side of my neck. What an asshole!

July 8th

Abby

An email from Holly came within an hour. It had the address and the real estate agent's information. I contacted him immediately and we set up an appointment for the next day.

The driveway was surrounded by large oak trees that formed a gorgeous canopy. The house was surrounded on all sides with trees and shrubs and flowers, giving the illusion that the rest of the town was miles away. The driveway was an old cobblestone, leading up to a two-stall garage.

The house itself was huge. It was beautifully designed to look like a cross between an old colonial home and a wood cabin. An odd combination, but it worked. It was obviously neglected, with missing shutters, broken glass on the windows, the foliage around completely overgrown, but it was still amazing.

My first thought was, *it's magnificent.* My second thought was, *holy shit, this house needs my help*. And my third thought was, *I'm going to live here.*

"Ms. Bradley?" The real estate agent approached as I stood and gawked at the house. "Paul Edwards."

"Nice to meet you, Mr. Edwards." I snapped out of my shock and shook his hand.

"Are you ready for the tour?" He gestured towards the house.

"Absolutely." I smiled and followed him inside.

The front door protested with a loud groan as he shoved it open. When we entered the large foyer, I gasped. There were holes in the floor and walls, there was wallpaper peeling everywhere, the floors were covered in dust and debris, broken furniture was everywhere.

I looked past all of that to the bones of the house, the huge open concept made it easy to picture a rustic kitchen, a butcher block island with stools, a six or eight person dining room table, couches and chairs surrounding the fireplace in the living room. I was instantly awestruck and ready to sign on the bottom line.

He gave me the full tour; there was a large pantry, a small

bathroom, an office/library, and a mudroom off the back door on the first floor. The second floor had two bedrooms with large en suite bathrooms and two bedrooms that shared a bathroom, jack-and-jill style. It was much bigger than I would need with just me and my baby, but I was enchanted.

We went back out to the cars, and Mr. Simon turned to me with a little smile. "I could tell you loved it."

"I definitely do," I admitted. "What's the listing price?"

"Well, I have to tell you, with the location and size of the lot, even in its current condition, market value is well over a half million." He smiled widely. "However, I've been instructed to make a one-time only offer to you for two hundred thousand."

"You're kidding!" I squealed. "Sold!"

He laughed loudly. "I thought you'd say that. Do you want to come to my office and we'll handle the pesky paperwork?"

"Yes, of course." I nodded and then looked at my watch. It was lunch time, and I'd really been trying to keep a regular eating schedule. In the past, I tended to skip meals when I got busy with work, but now that I was pregnant, I couldn't do that. "I'm just going to stop and grab something to eat, and I'll meet you there."

"No, no." He shook his head. "I'll call ahead to my secretary, and she'll have lunch waiting for us when we arrive. We'll have a working lunch. Compliments of Kade Barrett."

"Kade?" I tilted my head in confusion. "I thought his name was Kain."

"That's his brother," he told me casually. I didn't think much about it at the time, it was a family business. Obviously, Kain had spoken to me and Kade had spoken to Mr. Edwards, but they were both on the same page.

"All right." I smiled. "I'll follow you, then."

He smiled and got into his car.

Chapter 4

August 4th
Abby

"Four months," I told my contractor, Gus.

"You want the whole house done in four months?" he asked in shock. I didn't blame him, I almost never put demanding schedules on the guys I work with, but I was already four months pregnant and needed a home for us.

"The entire downstairs and at least the master suite upstairs needs to be complete," I instructed. "But I'm hoping we can get it all done. I'll hire more hands if you need them. I really need this one done."

"We'll get it done if you need it that bad," he assured me with a kind smile.

I'd always liked Gus. He was the kind of man a girl wishes to have as a father. He was in his late forties, laid back, laugh lines around his eyes, a bit of a dad-bod but still in good shape. He was kind and, most importantly, hard working.

We went over every inch of the house, and I told him my ideas. He smiled, nodded, took notes and made suggestions. We'd always worked well together, and I was grateful to have him as a contractor.

When I went back to my small apartment at the end of the day, I felt accomplished and satisfied. I logged onto my computer and started shopping online for baby stuff. I'd put them in storage until the house was ready.

I called my mother promptly at eight, knowing they'd just be finishing supper.

"Hello?" She always sounded confused when she answered the phone, which I never understood. Her caller ID told her it was me. Was she confused as to why I'd call her?

"Hi, Mom." I took a deep breath. "I was wondering if I could come for supper one day. I have something to tell you and Dad."

"Abby, you know I hate surprises," she chastised. "Just tell me now."

"I'm pregnant," I blurted.

"I'm assuming, since you felt the need to tell us, you're not getting an abortion?" she asked emotionlessly.

"No." I ground my teeth.

"Fine," she huffed. "I'll tell your father. Was there anything else?"

"Nope." I hung up without waiting for more. What had I expected? I didn't even know why I'd bothered. I'd only spoken to them a half a dozen times in the last five years, and none of those conversations had been especially pleasant either.

It was time to give up. If they didn't care to have a relationship with their daughter and grandchild, then why should I?

I crawled into bed feeling more alone than I ever had before.

August 5th

Abby

I parked my car on one of the busiest roads and started walking down the scenic neighborhood. Delicious smells poured from bakeries, knick-knacks decorated shop windows, moms pushed kids in strollers, shop owners waved at people walking by. A few people gave me curious glances or tentative smiles.

After the hints Kain Barrett had made on the phone about me taking interest in the community and working on future projects here, I decided to show myself around. I'd driven down the main streets multiple times this morning, just learning the area.

I woke up with a determination to put my best foot forward in my new life and move on from the past. I could make new friends and I had a baby coming. I would be fine, and touring the town was the perfect way to lift my spirits.

West Ridge was cosmetically no different than any other town, but something about it felt different, more close-knit, more comfortable, more… something I couldn't put my finger on.

"Ms. Bradley?" I turned towards the voice and inwardly groaned. It was the woman from the doctor's office, Lisa something, hustling down the sidewalk in front of a small boutique.

"What are you doing here?" I asked with trepidation, placing my hands on my hips and trying hard not to scowl at her. I had just started to feel better and now this.

"It's a coincidence. I promise I'm not stalking you, but we need to talk," she said with a frown as she stopped next to me on the sidewalk. "About your baby."

"Lady, I'm one minute away from calling the cops," I warned her, reaching into my purse for my phone.

"Then I have one minute to convince you not to," she said with a firm resolve. "You got pregnant by a bear, and you need to be aware of what your baby will be."

That stopped me cold. What the hell had she just said?

"What?" I narrowed my eyes and regarded her. "What the fuck does that even mean? I didn't have sex with a bear! And what do you mean, 'what my baby will be'?"

"Can we please talk?" she asked and gestured to the cafe down the street. "Maybe get a cup of coffee?"

I walked with her to the Bear Cave Cafe. It was a cozy place, clean and decorated with an old-world charm. Only a few people were seated around the dining room, mostly older couples. We found a table near the back and sat. A young waitress appeared immediately. Lisa ordered a black coffee, and I ordered a blueberry muffin and ice water. I'd already had my one daily allowance of coffee.

"All right, talk," I prompted Lisa once the waitress left.

"Do you read romance novels?" she asked me.

"No," I responded immediately, even though I had no idea what that had to do with anything.

"Do you know anything about shape-shifters?" she asked next.

I resisted the urge to roll my eyes. "Like werewolves?" I shrugged. "Only what I've seen on TV."

"Better than nothing," she sighed, fiddling with a napkin. "It's kind of like that, except these guys turn into bears."

"You're fucking with me, right?" I scoffed, not believing how ridiculous that sounded.

"Nope." She shook her head adamantly. "I can prove it to you, but first, the point is, that there's a seventy-five percent chance that your baby will be a bear-shifter, and you need to be prepared. You need to learn how to care for such a child and learn about the culture. And there's still the option of walking away, you can put the baby up for adoption and wash your hands of all of this."

"If you say the word *adoption* one more time, I'll reach across this table and slap you," I threatened, seriously getting pissed off.

She held her hands up defensively. "I'm just giving you options. You didn't ask for any of this, and you don't have to go through with it."

I mulled it over for a minute. I'd heard some of the rumors and gossip in Ridgewood about the happenings in West Ridge. I was doubtful, but not a complete non-believer.

"Let's say I believe you, just to move things along, what do you want me to do, exactly?"

"Well, I'd like to introduce you to another bear mom, she can teach you about their special needs," Lisa said enthusiastically, her eyes brightening as she spoke. "You are encouraged to stay in West Ridge. It's one of the largest bear communities in the country, and the perfect place to raise a bear cub. You'll be given a monthly stipend for your needs and the child's needs."

I held my hand up to stop her there. "A monthly stipend? Why? How much?"

"Ten thousand," she said nonchalantly, and I almost choked.

"What? From whom?" I forced out the words through my shock at the large amount. "You have a program to assist single bear mothers?"

"Not exactly." She pursed her lips, looking down at her hands on the table. "Your situation is... unique. Normally, when a bear finds his mate, they rarely separate. Divorce isn't common here."

"Mate?" I furrowed my eyebrows.

"Like a soul mate," she told me, looking up with a wistful look in her eyes. "A bear's mate is ingrained in them. When they meet, the connection is very powerful and hard to resist. Imagine the most intense sexual energy, combined with the need to possess and protect, combined with the need to love and cherish."

I squirmed uncomfortably in my seat, trying not to draw the wrong conclusions, but fearing that I already had. "Are you saying that I'm this bear's mate?"

She glanced at the bite mark on my neck and grimaced. I gasped, covering the spot with my hand.

He'd rejected me. He had an intense 'mate' connection to me and instead of wanting to love and protect me, he fucked me, knocked me up and left me for someone else to deal with. Fury boiling in my blood, I shot out of the chair.

"This conversation is over," I turned and marched out of the cafe. I didn't even care that I hadn't eaten or paid. Let her pay for my muffin. She could eat it too for all I cared. I'd find something else.

"Ms. Bradley, wait!" Lisa called behind me. I heard her heels clicking on the tile and resisted the urge to run. "We have so much more to talk about."

She grabbed my elbow, and I wheeled around.

"Not right now," I snapped and leveled her with a glare. "I have enough to think about. If what you say about the bear thing is true, then I'll accept I have things to learn before giving birth, but I need a minute. We can talk again another day."

"Fine," she said reluctantly. "I'll be in touch."

She handed me a business card, and I shoved it in my purse.

"Can't wait," I said sarcastically and turned away from her. I walked out of the cafe and down the street to my car, driving straight to the new house.

When I pulled into the yard, there was a fucking bear standing on the east side of the house near the garage. It was huge, dark brown and just walking through my yard. I slammed on the brakes as he looked at me with an eerie intelligence. His bright yellow eyes locked on mine and he tipped his head. My heart pounded erratically as we maintained eye contact. Then, he turned and strolled off into the trees.

As far-fetched as it was, I considered myself an open-minded person and after seeing *that*, I believed it. I wondered who the bear was. Just a neighbor checking out the progress on the house? Or someone else?

I suddenly had a hundred questions, and I needed to make a list before I called Lisa.

Kade

I was weak. Kit was weak. I couldn't eat, I barely slept. I had trouble concentrating at work, or on anything, really. My mind was consumed with thoughts of her, remembering our night together and wondering how she was handling the pregnancy.

I needed to see her. Even just a glimpse was enough. I was disappointed when I got to the house and she wasn't there, she'd been there almost every day. I knew because so had I.

I would never admit it, not even to Kain, but I'd been getting weaker and more restless over the last several weeks. Each day seemed to be worse than the last, until I finally caved and came to check on her. As soon as I saw her, my bear grew stronger and calmer. Now, I couldn't seem to stay away.

When she pulled into the driveway, our eyes met for the first time since that night. Blood pounded through my veins, and I wanted to roar my elation.

She was like my drug, and I needed my fix. I didn't know how my dad survived as long as he did after my mom left. I couldn't imagine the pain, the heartache, the loss. I didn't want to imagine it, that was the problem. Mates bring nothing but disaster.

I jogged back to where I left my clothes, quickly shifted back to my human form and got dressed. Kain would never let me hear the end of it if he knew what I was doing. I couldn't make myself stop though, I ached for her.

When I got back to the office, Kain was perched on the edge of my desk, waiting for me. I sighed, knowing full well what he wanted to talk about.

"She's keeping the baby," he announced when I'd closed the door. "I just talked to Lisa. She didn't believe the bear thing right away, but Lisa said she didn't completely reject it either. I like her. She's feisty."

"So you've told me," I responded with annoyance. "Now get off my desk and do some work."

"She plans to move into Greenhope before she delivers," he continued, ignoring me. "Lisa is going to introduce her to Missy Parker."

I nodded. Missy had six cubs, and if anyone could teach a new mother about raising bears, it was her. I moved around my desk and sat in my cushy leather executive chair.

"Are you sure you only want to give her ten grand a month?" he asked, for the third time. "You could afford a lot more."

"We talked about this," I reminded him, handing him a file on an urban development project. "It's more than enough for a nanny, food and expenses. It has to seem like it's a charitable contribution, not child support. It's a lot of money to some people."

"Not you," he snorted, setting the file down without looking at it.

"It's enough so she wouldn't have to work if she didn't want to," I told him. "Especially with her income properties and investments."

"Fine," he relented, looking out the large bay window behind me. "I wonder if it's a boy or a girl."

"What are you doing?" I asked, exasperated, snatching up the same file and smacking him in the chest with it until he took it. My own thoughts were bad enough without him adding to them. "Are you trying to torture me?"

"It's not my fault," he huffed, finally glancing down at the file and standing up, raising his ass off my desk. "You could be with her right now, picking out wallpaper or some shit. Don't be pissy with me just because you're an asshole."

I scowled at him, and he threw his hands up, obviously as annoyed with me as I was with myself. He turned to leave but then leveled me with a hard look.

"Have you considered what's going to happen when you run into her?" He voiced the same question I'd been trying to answer myself for weeks. "West Ridge isn't that big. One day, you'll bump into her. It's unavoidable. What are you going to say? What are you going to say to your kid?"

Okay, so my plan had some major flaws. I was well aware. He smirked at my silence and walked out of my office.

It hadn't even been six months, and I was already reconsidering my plan. It had been a decent idea at the time, I thought; get her out of my system, get my heir, move on. I hadn't expected it to be so intense that I'd mark her and complete the bond, sealing me to her forever. I hadn't expected her to keep the child and move into my town. I definitely hadn't thought things through, and now I needed a new plan.

I needed her. I needed my cub. I was going to have to go see her. At least talk to her. But what the hell did I say? *Sorry for knocking you up on purpose?*

I dropped my head into my hands. I royally fucked this one up.

Nothing else mattered anymore, I had to do something. I couldn't live my life sneaking around just to catch a glimpse of her every day.

What the hell was I supposed to do?

Chapter 5

August 25th
Abby

After checking on my current projects, and spending the rest of the morning at the house supervising, I met Lisa in town for lunch.

"All right." She got right to it after we'd placed our orders. "We're going over to Missy's house after lunch and my nephew agreed to shift into his bear for you, as proof."

"That's not necessary," I sighed. "I believe you."

"Great, but what changed your mind?" She tilted her head at me curiously.

I looked around, checking for eavesdroppers and then spoke in a low voice. "I saw a bear."

She just stared back at me, without blinking.

"In town," I continued, feeling she wanted more explanation. "At my house. He looked at me, and I don't know… he just had this intelligence in his eyes, and… well, I believe you."

I squirmed in my seat, uncomfortable by her silence and my confession.

"Huh," was all she said.

I rolled my eyes.

"Well." She took a sip of water, and finally eased the strange awkwardness. "My nephew will still shift for you if you want to see it. It's really something. I'm glad you're taking it so well."

"Do you have any idea who it could have been?" I asked tentatively.

She shook her head slowly with a deep frown. "That's one of the reasons I was stumped. Most of the guys go up to Eagle Crest to shift and run." She referred to the mountain range just outside of West Ridge.

"We don't usually see bears in town," she continued. "Unless they're cubs, sometimes the little ones shift unintentionally with high emotions."

"Oh." I sipped my water and then leaned back quickly as the waitress appeared, placing my club sandwich in front of me and a chicken Caesar salad in front of Lisa.

I took a few minutes to just eat and enjoy the crisp flavors of my meal while I pondered my situation. Then I remembered what she said.

"What's the other reason you were stumped?" I asked her.

She looked away. "Caught that, did you?"

"Yes."

"I mean, it's just not something we see every day, is it?" She huffed and struggled to explain it, but it felt like she was hiding something. "The bears are actually men, and some women, and they don't go wandering around other people's yards. If they're curious about their neighbors, they walk up and say hello, as a man, not a bear."

"What does this mean?" I pointed to the prominent mark on my neck, even though I had a good idea.

"It's a mate's mark," Lisa answered, blushing and looking down intently at her salad. "When a bear finds his mate, he bites her, marking her, as a way of accepting the mate and sealing the bond for life."

That didn't sit right at all. He accepted me, but he rejected me. It didn't make sense.

"I don't understand," I said weakly, more to myself than her.

"Your situation is just… unique." She looked at me apologetically. "I don't know what to say about that."

We fell into a tense silence again, I still couldn't wrap my mind around everything. I accepted the *bear* thing, but I didn't understand the *man*.

What was it about me that had made him decide to fuck me and forget me? Did he realize the consequences his actions had wrought? Did he know about any of this? Did he care at all?

I didn't even understand why I was so obsessed about it. I'd only had the one night with him, and although it was easily the most amazing sex of my life, I didn't know anything about him. I knew the way he brought my body to life, I knew how amazing his touch felt, I knew how my entire body seemed to explode with euphoria when I came, but that was all just sex. Why did he still have me so crazy? Why did I miss him? How could I be stupid enough to miss the asshole who had put me in this situation?

"Can I ask you a question?" Lisa asked suddenly.

I nodded absently as I chewed my sandwich.

"What did it feel like?" She leaned in, excitement and curiosity bubbling in her eyes.

"What?"

"The mate bond." She leaned in even further. "They say it's incredibly intense for the bear, but even the human can feel it. Did you feel it?"

I thought back, remembering every touch, every sensation, every tingle. It actually explained a lot that it was caused by some mythical bond.

"As soon as I heard his voice, I got goosebumps." I looked down, staring at my plate, but actually seeing my stranger's eyes, lips, hands. "It felt like nothing I'd ever experienced before with my ex-boyfriend. I didn't know it could be like that."

"And when he kissed you?" Her eyes were so bright with romantic notions, I almost hated to dash them.

"He didn't." I cleared my throat and held my head high. "We never kissed."

She gasped in a little breath, her eyes filling with such sympathy and sorrow, I had to look away. I didn't want her pity.

After lunch, Lisa drove me to meet Missy, a woman in her late thirties, with bright red hair, who'd just had her sixth bear cub. Lisa said a quick hello to Missy, and then said she had an errand to run, and left me alone in a stranger's house.

"Don't stand on ceremony, girl. Come on in." Missy waved me into her cluttered house. Toys and clothes covered almost every surface.

"If you want to sit down, you have to fold some clothes." Missy gestured to the couch, heaping with clothes. "It's laundry day, and I've been washing up a storm, but between Libby's soccer practice, Timmy's baseball practice, Krissy wanting to have a tea party and Johnny always wanting the boob, I haven't had time to fold."

I was confused and slightly horrified, until she pointed to the baby in a swinging chair, and I realized that must be Johnny.

"Is this a bad time?" I asked tentatively as I walked slowly into the room. "I could come back later?"

"Pffth." Missy made an amused noise of dismissal. "It

doesn't get any better. And the kids don't have any events for the next couple of hours, so really, now is best."

"O-kay." I drew out the word, and then started folding clothes, because I didn't want to stand there like an idiot. I'd never been openly friendly, and I wasn't comfortable, but I was here to learn.

"All right, so Lisa told me to tell you the basics in raising cubs, so I'm just going to talk, and you can stop me if you want to or if you have questions."

And talk she did. Missy went on and on about the similarities and differences of raising children and raising cubs. She had six children: Bobby Jr. was twelve, Reggie was eleven, Libby was eight, Timmy was six, Krissy was four, and Johnny was nine months. The older four were all cubs. Timmy had recently shifted for the first time. Krissy was too young to tell.

Apparently, there's a seventy-five percent chance a baby born of a bear will be a cub. Because if it's a boy, it'll definitely be a cub, but if it's a girl, there's a fifty/fifty chance.

Missy's parents had both been bears, but she was human. According to her, she was in the unlucky half of that gamble. Her husband, Bobby Sr. worked as the chief operating officer of Bare Industries, which was a godsend because with a lesser job they wouldn't have been able to afford to keep having kids. She'd always wanted ten children, so they'd started as soon as they got married at twenty.

"Raising cubs isn't all that different to raising children, I imagine," she'd said. "The biggest thing is making sure to plan lots of trips to the mountains so they can practice shifting and get lots of exercise. We go every week. And they need more protein. Oh, and you really have to watch out for high emotions, because they could shift unintentionally and tear up your house. This one time, with Bobby Jr., he was about seven..."

And on she went with a story about how Bobby Jr. had shifted in the house when his Xbox froze.

And I folded clothes. I had a tea party with Krissy. I held Johnny. I folded more clothes. I helped Missy make supper. And I listened to every word as Missy talked and talked. When Johnny cried, she never missed a beat in her talking as she changed him and fed him. I got the feeling she didn't get a lot of adult interaction, and she didn't even care that the conversation was mostly one-sided.

She asked me a few questions about my pregnancy, which I answered politely. She asked me a few questions about the baby's father, which I avoided neatly by asking a question of my own. I caught her looking at my bite mark once, and noticed her own, significantly more subtle mark.

Lisa finally returned, just as I was questioning whether or not I was going to have to find alternative transportation. Missy gave me her phone number in case I wanted to chat. We said goodbye and thanked Missy.

"Did you have fun?" Lisa asked once we were settled in the car, sounding like a mom picking her kid up from a playdate.

"Missy was nice," I answered. "I learned a lot."

"Good." She nodded as she navigated the car. "Do you have any questions?"

"Not right now, I think Missy answered all of my immediate questions, and I haven't had time to process anything else."

Lisa dropped me off at my car, and I drove to the house to see what kind of progress Gus and the team had made today.

Kade

. . .

My skin felt too tight, and I was antsy as fuck, she wasn't at the house today, and I missed seeing her. I scratched at my arms and rubbed at my chest, my breathing labored, my heartbeat erratic. Where was she? What was she doing? Was she safe? Was she with someone?

Was she with another man?

Somewhere deep down, I knew I was being irrational and crazy, but I couldn't control it. Kit was just below the surface, dying to break free and tear the city apart to find her.

Mate! He screamed in my head, pacing incessantly. *I want to see her! She's mine! Mate. Mate. Mate.*

It was never ending, but worse than ever today.

It was nearing the end of the workday when my cell phone rang, *Missy*. That was strange, Missy had never called me before. We had each other's numbers, as acquaintances, her husband was second in command after Kain and me. Kain had said Lisa was taking Abby to meet Missy. Abby!

I answered the phone quickly, before it occurred to me that Missy didn't know I was connected to Abby in any way, and Missy immediately started talking. I liked Missy, she was friendly and open, but the woman could sure talk.

"Hi Kade. Am I catching you at a bad time? I had the most interesting afternoon. Lisa brought over a young woman to talk about raising cubs, she's a first-time mom, you know? And she was just the prettiest girl, blonde hair, blue eyes, gorgeous. Kind of quiet, didn't say much, not that I minded. I can talk enough for an entire dinner party, as you know. I liked her anyway. Did you know she folded six baskets of laundry while she was here, and she picked up toys, and she helped me make supper?"

I sat back in my chair and sighed, fairly certain Abby was all right and now understanding where she had been today. I sat quietly as Missy continued without pausing for a breath.

"Krissy just loved her, they had a tea party and she told

Krissy that she didn't like sugar in her tea because sugar was bad for you and gave your teeth sugar bugs, and now Krissy doesn't want sugar! Can you imagine! The woman is a godsend. I wish I'd thought of that. Of course, it's different coming from a parent. Kids never listen to their parents. But anyways, I'm off topic... So, I asked Abby about the father of her baby, and do you know what she said?"

My heart skipped a beat, they'd talked about me? Did Abby know it was me? Did Missy? My tongue stuck to the roof of my mouth. Luckily, Missy didn't care to wait for a response.

"She said, if you're still planning on having ten kids, you're going to need a bigger house. She turned it right back to me and got me talking again! But you know I don't miss much, even if I never shut up. And there's only two men in the world that Lisa could be working for, and well, I just don't believe it would be Kain."

She paused, probably waiting to see if I would confirm or deny. I didn't do either, which apparently confirmed it for her.

"That's what I thought." She harrumphed loudly. "Abby is great, Kade. I don't know what you're up to, but I can tell that something stinks here. Her mark was way darker than any I've seen before. What the hell were you trying to do? Bite her head off? You're a good man under that gruff exterior, I know because Bobby respects you, and he's not the easiest man to win over."

Bobby had been with our company longer than Kain and I. He hadn't known what to expect when we took over for our dad, and we'd really shaken the place up. It had taken time, several successful business ventures, many hours of meetings and finally, a round of beer at the bar downtown before Bobby had smiled at us and told us that he was glad we were there to do some good.

"Kade, just listen to me, okay?" Missy's voice softened

through the phone. "I don't know what's going on, but I can imagine. I know you don't have the best example, but don't hurt her. And don't hurt yourself. Neither of you deserve that kind of pain."

There was a loud crash in the background and she started yelling. "Timothy Roger! You knock that off this instant. Don't put that in your sister's ear!" She quickly spoke to me. "I have to go, Kade. Call me if you need a verbal ass-kicking." And she hung up.

I blew out a hard breath of air and chuckled softly. That was Missy for you, always called them like she saw them and didn't apologize for who she was. And she'd liked Abby. I went over everything Missy had said about her, and then there was a knock at my door.

I glanced at the clock, everyone should be leaving for the day. "Come in."

Lisa marched into my office, a purposeful look on her face, stood right in front of my desk, and balled her fists onto her hips.

"I won't do it anymore, Kade! I won't lie to her! She doesn't deserve it."

"Why have you been lying to her?" I frowned, not understanding.

Lisa was supposed to be introducing Abby to the community, as the daughter of two bears who'd lived in West Ridge all her life, nobody was more qualified than Lisa. Also, I didn't trust many people like I did Lisa.

She scoffed loudly. "What was I supposed to say when she asked me if I knew why there would be a *bear* in her yard?"

I flinched.

"What was I supposed to say when she asked what her mark meant?" She scowled at me. "I told her the truth, I hate lying, but I left out the details. Like the fact I knew her mate personally, and he's a world-class numbskull."

I stared at her flatly, even while I wanted to kick my own ass, and I was on the verge of crawling out of my skin. I didn't want Lisa to see how badly I was affected. I didn't want anyone to see.

She narrowed her eyes at me and leaned forward, fists braced on my desk. "I don't know who you think you're fooling with that stoic bullshit, but it isn't me. I saw her mark, remember? It looks like you were trying to bite clean through her. You figure out your shit, Kade Barrett, because if she ever decides to ask me point blank if I know who you are, I'm going to tell her everything and… hell, I'll march her straight up here!"

She stood and glared at me for a full minute, while I sat there like a big dummy and gaped at her. I'd never seen Lisa so pissed off before. She was normally very professional and mild-mannered. She turned on her heel and stomped out of my office.

"Lisa!" I called after her before she could leave.

She glanced over her shoulder at me.

"Thanks." It was really all I could say.

She nodded and closed the door gently behind her.

I stood up, straightened my jacket and tie, knowing exactly what I had to do. It was undeniable, and unavoidable.

My office door burst open as I was reaching for it, and Kain strode in, a hard expression on his face. He startled when he saw me standing just inside the door.

"Enough is enough, Kade," he began.

"Get out." I pushed him towards the door. "I'm going."

"Going where?" he regarded me curiously as he allowed me to push him out the door.

"Since everyone seems to have ganged up against me, I guess I don't have much choice." It was a shitty excuse, and not remotely true, but I was still adamant about not admitting my own shortcomings. Nobody needed to know just how pathetic and desperate I'd become in such a short amount of time.

"What are you going to say?" He put his hand on my arm to stop my forward advance.

"I don't know," I sighed. I mean, honestly, what did someone say after being a complete and utter shithead to someone who was destined to be their fucking soul mate?

I ran my hands through my hair. If I could go back and kick my ass, I would. I never should have approached her to begin with, I should've just tried to ignore the fact that I'd found my mate.

It was too late now, though. I'd gone through with my convoluted plan, and now it was time to reap the consequences.

Chapter 6

August 25th
Abby

I'd been home for five minutes when there was a knock on my door. I frowned, I never got visitors. I lifted my tired body from the couch and walked to the door. Who knew folding clothes and having tea parties could take so much out of a person? I looked out the peephole at the perfectly styled hair as he looked down and groaned.

"What are you doing here?" I yelled through the door.

"I need to talk to you, Abby," Simon said. "Open the door."

"No. I don't want to see you. We're over." I put my hands on my slightly swollen belly. I wasn't embarrassed by it, I actually thought my little bump was cute and bought special maternity clothes to highlight it, but I didn't want him to see it.

"Come on, Abby. I said I was sorry." He knocked on the door again. "It wasn't how it looked. Just let me explain."

"It looked like you were fucking Liam on your kitchen table," I ground out. "What part of that wasn't how it looked?"

"I don't want to get into it while I'm in the hallway," he whispered loudly enough for me to hear. "Open the door so we can talk."

"Go away, Simon." I frowned at the door.

I had thought I was done with this shit. I hadn't gotten any texts from him in months. Naturally, I'd assumed he had moved on. I definitely had.

"Not until I talk to you," he replied.

"She said go away," a deep voice growled.

I recognized it instantly and just like the first time I'd heard it, goosebumps erupted on my skin. *It couldn't be.*

"Fuck off, dude," Simon said to him. "This is none of your business."

I heard a loud thump and ripped the door open to see my stranger holding Simon against the wall, one hand on his throat, his eyes full of fury.

"It is my business," he growled. "I don't want to see you anywhere near her ever again."

"Let him go." I pulled at his arm, my hand tingling from the contact, but he ignored me. Simon's face was turning red from lack of oxygen, I needed to do something before he passed out. I squeezed his bicep, my hand not even wrapping halfway around the large muscle, and spoke softly, "Daddy, let go."

My stranger turned to look at me, his eyes almost neon yellow and moving over me with an intense possessiveness that made me shiver. He released Simon abruptly, turning fully to face me, his eyes fading into a yellow green. Simon staggered against the wall, coughing and wheezing.

"Abby," Simon gasped, looking pointedly at my belly. "You're pregnant?"

I watched in fascination as my stranger's eyes glowed yellow, and he turned his attention back to Simon. I quickly stepped between them.

"It's not yours," I told Simon. "You need to leave."

"Are you sure?" Simon asked, glancing from me to my stranger skeptically.

"Leave!" He moved to step around me, but I moved with him, firmly planting myself between them before he could do any more damage.

Simon frowned, giving me one last look, as he turned and walked down the hall. I sighed and walked into my apartment, not bothering to see what my stranger did. I couldn't decide if I was more angry with him for everything he had done – add trying to kill Simon to the list – or if I was more happy to see him again which was ridiculous because I barely knew him.

A thousand questions jumbled in my mind, but my body sang with acute awareness of him, and I couldn't sort out my thoughts. I knew it was the mate bond, trying to control me, but I had to be stronger.

I could feel him as he followed me and closed the door. I can't explain why I wasn't worried about him being in my apartment. I just knew he wouldn't hurt me.

"What are you doing here?" I asked tiredly, sitting on my couch and curling my legs up under me.

"I need to talk to you," he said, lowering himself onto the couch beside me, placing his hand firmly on my leg. I tried to scoot away, but he pulled me even closer.

"What are you doing?" I tried to push his hand off my leg, and his fingers tightened around my thigh. I want to say I was pushing him away out of discomfort, but the truth is, his touch gave me pleasant sensations in very intimate places.

"Abby," he growled, low and guttural.

"What?" I turned to meet his eyes, which were still almost completely yellow and his pupils were huge. His breathing was labored and he looked pained, like he was having an internal struggle. It was riveting to see, but also a little scary.

"Are you okay?" I ask hesitantly.

He pulled me into his lap suddenly and buried his face in my neck, breathing deeply. He nuzzled my neck and a rumbling purr vibrated through his chest. I wanted to melt against him and bask in his rugged manly scent, but I held myself firmly in check, remaining aloof as I perched on his lap.

I knew I should be pissed at him and push him away, but I couldn't bring myself to do it. Something told me that he needed me, and for some reason, my heart went out to him. My body's profound response to him didn't help me either. Before he arrived, I had a million questions to ask him, but just then, I couldn't think of one.

After several minutes sitting like that, he started nibbling on my neck. It felt incredible, and I wanted to just give in to him, but my pride wouldn't let me. I pulled away and looked at his eyes. They were more green than yellow again, and his pupils had constricted back to normal. His breathing evened out and he looked more relaxed.

"Why are you here?" I asked again.

"To talk," he answered finally, but tightened his hold on my waist when I tried to climb off him.

His hand slid to my swollen belly, and I froze. I narrowed my eyes at him as I summoned all my pain.

"What could you possibly have to say to me now?" I scowled. "Sorry for knocking you up, Abby. Sorry for not telling you I'm a bear, Abby. Oh! Sorry for rejecting you as my mate, Abby."

He winced and his grip on me loosened. I took the opportunity and pushed off his lap, getting some much needed space.

"I think you should leave," I said softly, needing distance from him so I could think.

"You don't understand," he told me.

"Damn right I don't!" I snapped. "This is bullshit! You're a fucking bear! You got me pregnant! You fucking bit me! And now you're here, trying to kill my ex-boyfriend, and holding me like you have any right to..."

I'd sort of gone off on a tirade but luckily, he interrupted me.

"Can you just let me fucking talk?" He glared at me and stood up, uncurling to his full height, making me look up at him. He reached out to touch my arm.

"No!" I shrieked and slapped him across the cheek.

He looked almost as surprised as I was. I couldn't have him touching me right now, the tingles were too alluring and would distract me from my anger.

"Don't touch me," I said through clenched teeth.

"It's not me!" he roared suddenly.

I took a step back, instinctively wrapping my arms around my belly, as his breathing became heavy and his eyes turned yellow again.

"It's my damn bear."

I didn't know what to say to that. I didn't know enough about it. When I didn't comment, he took a deep breath and ran a hand through his hair, gripping it and making it stick up wildly.

"He's weak," he admitted softly. "Being near you helps."

His eyes slowly faded back to the green-yellow hue. It was mesmerizing to watch, like when the sky changed colors with the sunrise.

"Why is he weak?" I asked hesitantly, not sure I wanted to know the answer, not sure I wanted to care.

"Because of you," he sighed, and I narrowed my eyes at him. He held his hands up. "I'm not blaming you. I'm an asshole, I know. It's my fault."

I nodded. At least he was aware of that.

"What do you want?" I asked, deciding to just skip to the bottom line.

"I don't know." He frowned and turned away from me, looking out the window of my small apartment. "I've never wanted a mate. I thought if I fucked you once I would be okay to just leave it at that."

"But?" I crossed my arms over my chest and waited.

He turned back to me, a sheepish look on his too handsome face.

"But then I marked you." His eyes flicked to my neck, and I reflexively covered the bite mark with my hand. "It sealed our bond and guaranteed I can't live without you."

"Then why did you do it?" I asked curiously. "Will you die?"

"No, I won't die," he sighed, and ran his hands through his hair again. "I'll just be weak and struggling with my bear constantly, slowly going crazy."

He was here because his bear was craving me, craving his mate, the bond. He wasn't there for me, I realized. I opened the door and gestured for him to leave.

"Please go," I begged quietly.

Hurt and frustration flashed in his eyes. I looked away from him and held the door open.

"Can I come back?" he asked quietly.

"Why?" I didn't look at him. I couldn't.

"To see you." He took a step towards me, and I cowered.

He flinched back at my reaction. I wasn't scared of him, I was scared of my reaction to him.

"To see the baby," he added, and my heart broke in a whole new way.

The baby.

The baby that I'd resigned would grow up without a father. The baby whose father was standing in front of me.

I slammed the door and poked him in the chest. I wanted to shout at him, but I couldn't do it properly because I didn't know anything about him.

"What's your name?" I yelled instead.

"Kade." He winced. "Kade Barrett."

Oh, holy fuck. It all connected in my head. The house, the money. He did all of it. He knew the whole time.

I slapped him, hard. He didn't flinch. I slapped him again. I punched his chest. Tears flowed down my face as I pounded my fists against his chest.

"You asshole!" I screamed. "You did this on purpose!"

"Fuck, Abby," he said as he stood and took my beating. "I'm sorry!"

"It's not good enough!" I wailed and pushed him away from me. "Get out!"

"Baby, listen…" he started, but I cut him off.

"Don't call me that!" I pushed him again and again. "Get out! How could you? You're worse than him! You wanted me to forget his name? Now I need to forget yours! Go!"

He grabbed my arms at the mention of Simon and his eyes flashed yellow.

"I'll go," he said slowly, his voice low and growly. "But if I see him here again, I'll kill him. No man touches you. You're mine."

"You're the one who rejected me, you dick!" I kicked him in the shin.

He grunted and spun me around, wrapping my arms around me and holding me in place.

"Fuck you, Kade Barrett! I hate you!"

He released me abruptly, and I stumbled forward. He grabbed my arms to steady me. I flailed and pulled away from him, before I collapsed into a heap on the floor, tears flowing down my face.

He knelt next to me and tried to help me up. I swatted his hands away.

"Stop fighting me, damn it!" he roared.

"No," I sobbed out. "I can't."

"Yes, you can," he said softly and wiped a strand of hair off my face.

I flinched, but I didn't try to stop him. He wiped the tears from my cheek with his thumb. Fresh tears immediately replaced them.

"I'm so sorry, Abby." He sat down next to me and rubbed my back. "I know I'm an asshole. I wasn't thinking straight. I didn't know you'd be like this."

"Like what?" I sniffed. "An emotional wreck? That's the pregnancy hormones. I'm not usually like this."

"No," he chuckled softly, brushing my hair off my shoulder and then continued rubbing my back. "I meant I didn't know you'd be so strong. I didn't know you'd stay in the community, and keep the baby."

All the times Lisa mentioned adoption echoed in my brain, and I just knew. He'd pulled the strings on everything, from the very beginning.

"Oh, God." I covered my face with my hands. "It was you. You were going to adopt the baby."

His hand stilled on my back and he stayed quiet, confirming my suspicion.

"What the fuck were you thinking coming here?" Anger surged through me, I wiped my face and rose quickly from the floor, ignoring my protesting body. "Did you think I'd be happy that you're here now? You think you're going to take care of me and it'll all be wonderful?"

"I don't know." He rose and met my heated glare with a

sad, tired look. "I know I messed up. Can you let me try to apologize, at least?"

"It won't do any good," I said resolutely. "You did this. You can't undo it."

"I wouldn't want to," he replied automatically, then flinched at my appalled expression.

"I would do things differently if I could," he amended. "But I don't regret fucking you. I don't regret making you pregnant."

I huffed a little, and he gave me a soft smile.

"You look so beautiful pregnant with my baby." His sweet words soothed my aching heart, but I couldn't let myself give in to him. "I didn't know I'd feel like this, Abby. I didn't know I wouldn't be able to stop thinking about you. I didn't know I'd admire you."

"You don't need to say all that," I sighed in resignation. "If you want to see the baby, I'll let you. We can do joint custody."

I turned away from him and walked into the kitchen for a glass of water, just to do something, to get away from him, to breathe and think.

"What if I want to see you?" he asked, following me into the kitchen.

I took a big gulp of water to give myself a minute to process and debate his words. I set the glass down and braced my hands on the edge of the sink.

I didn't care about my body's reaction to him, I was too confused and mad to give him any hope. "I'm angry and I'm damaged. If you need to see me for your bear or whatever, look with your eyes. But I need you to stay away from me."

He didn't respond so I turned my head to see him. He looked torn and pained, but nodded when he saw me watching him.

"You tell me if you need anything, okay?" he said. "More

money, someone to drive you to the doctor, anything you want, it's yours."

"I don't want the money at all," I frowned and turned to face him, crossing my arms over my chest.

"You will take it," he growled, taking a step towards me.

"I'm not an idiot," I snapped. "I'll take the money for child support. Which is what it is, right?"

He winced.

"Throw some money at her, give her a house and it'll be all right," I mocked, still feeling righteously pissed off.

"The house was Kain's idea when you were determined to keep the baby," he told me quietly.

"Well, then, tell him thank you. I actually love the house," I admitted with a huff.

"It was my grandparents'," he said with the barest hint of a smile twitching the corner of his lips. "I inherited it."

"You gave me your inheritance?" I gasped. "The house should stay in your family."

"It is." He glanced down at my belly.

"Oh." I rubbed my little bump instinctively. "You and Kain didn't want it?"

"No," he said. "We both have apartments near the office. Neither of us had the patience to do the work it required. But I hear it's right up your alley."

I smiled softly. "It is, actually. It'll be beautiful when I'm done with it."

"I'm sure." He nodded once.

A silence fell between us, and I wasn't sure what to say. I drank the rest of my water and put the glass in the dishwasher.

"Look, Abby," he started slowly. "I understand you're pissed at me. I know you hate me. I'll try to stay away from you. I'm not saying I'll be great at it, because it's physically painful, but I'll try if that's what you want."

I remained quiet as I absorbed his words. I watched the emotions play across his face, his eyes a bright green with just the usual yellow surrounding his iris.

"I know it's not fair to you to say this," he hesitated before pushing on, "but if I see you with that guy again, or any man, I might not be able to control myself."

"I really want to be angry enough to slap you again," I admitted as I narrowed my eyes at him. "That possessiveness is bullshit considering what you've done to me."

I paused as I let him feel the weight of my words, and then I gave him a break. "But the truth is, I have no interest in Simon or any other man, so it won't be a problem. I know you have some weird bear bonding problem you're struggling with, and while I don't completely understand it, I won't hold it against you."

"And you won't let him come back?" he pushed.

"I didn't know he'd show up today," I told him. "We broke up before I met you, after I caught him with my friend, Liam. I will never go back to him. If he shows up again, I'll send him away again, but I doubt he will after today."

He nodded and handed me a business card. I glanced down to see his name and information.

"In case you need anything," he said. "My cell is on the back."

"Okay." I nodded and put the card on the counter.

"Um..." he hesitated, looking strangely uncomfortable. "Are you going to find out if it's a boy or a girl?"

My heart flipped over in my chest. He looked ridiculously cute when he was awkward, which should be outlawed on a man who was already incredibly sexy. I worried my bottom lip, trying to force my mind back to the conversation.

"My ultrasound is next week," I replied.

He still looked uncomfortable, and I felt sorry for him. He

did this all wrong and he hurt me, but maybe there was more to it.

The words were out of my mouth before I could think twice. "Would you like to come?"

Surprise and relief flashed across his face, he reached a handout to me, but then quickly caught himself and dropped it.

"Really?" he asked. "Are you sure?"

"Only if you want to." I shrugged, trying to appear unaffected.

"I would like that," he said softly. "A lot."

"Okay then." I gave him a weak smile.

Chapter 7

September 1st
Kade

It was the day of the ultrasound and we were going to be late if she didn't leave soon. I was sitting in the tree line, watching and waiting. I didn't even know why since I knew I'd see her soon, but it had become a habit. But now, it was time to leave for the doctor and she was still in the house with the construction workers.

It was the end of summer, and the leaves were already beginning to fade into yellow. I couldn't wait for her to see this place in the fall. It was quite spectacular, and I bet she'd appreciate it.

I heard a loud crash, and I had to fight the urge to run inside. I doubted a bear barreling through the house would help matters.

She ran out a second later.

"I'll be back soon!" she called over her shoulder. She

turned and ran towards her car. She caught a glimpse of me and froze. Our eyes locked, and I sat on my haunches so she understood I wasn't a threat.

"Kade?" she asked cautiously.

I tilted my head in acknowledgement.

"We're going to be late," she told me needlessly.

I nodded and turned to run to where I left my clothes. I shifted quickly, got dressed and sped to the doctor's office. I met her there as she was walking in.

"Why have you been watching my house?" she asked as we entered. "The guys have mentioned seeing you."

I grunted in response because I didn't have a good excuse. She rolled her eyes at me.

"I told you I was weak," I offered lamely after she checked in and sat down next to me. I fought the powerful urge to reach over and take her hand.

I couldn't believe I'd been reduced to this, and I was beyond angry with myself, but I couldn't take it out on her either. I'd already put her through enough.

We sat quietly until her name was called. She jumped up, and I stood awkwardly beside her, more unsure of myself than I'd been my entire life. She followed the nurse, and I followed her. I felt like a puppy, awkward and uncoordinated. I wanted to kick my own ass, I wanted to run out of the uncomfortable situation, but I also didn't want to leave her side, and I was excited to see the ultrasound.

The nurse checked her weight and blood pressure and then told her to change into a hospital gown before leaving us. Abby looked at the gown and then at me in alarm.

"Don't ask me to leave," I demanded, just to tease her. "I wouldn't mind a show."

"You're an ass," she said, but she couldn't hide the little grin. "Close your eyes."

I crossed my arms over my chest in defiance and kept my

eyes wide open. If she wasn't kicking me out, there was no way I was missing it. She huffed and turned her back to me, pulling her shirt over her head. I groaned at the sight of her smooth skin, the curve of her hips, the hint of pregnant belly that I could see.

As she reached back to unhook her bra, I had to bite down on my lip until I tasted blood and clench my fists tight to keep from reaching for her. She pulled on the hospital gown quickly and covered her beauty from my greedy gaze.

She struggled with the ties, and I jumped up to assist her. I tied them effortlessly, and she gave me a shy smile over her shoulder.

"Thank you," she said.

"You're welcome." I smacked her ass playfully, desperate to ease some of the awkward tension between us.

She jumped and giggled. The sound was like music and soothed my frazzled nerves.

I sat back down, and she slipped her pants off.

"Fuck," I breathed out as I took in her long, shapely legs.

"Stop making everything dirty," she scolded me.

"I can't help it when you're undressing in front of me!" I said defensively.

"I had to change into the hospital gown," she reminded me. "I told you to close your eyes."

"I could never close my eyes while you're undressing," I confessed.

She smirked and opened her mouth to say something, then blushed and snapped it closed, looking away from me quickly. I wondered what she was about to say when someone knocked on the door and pushed it open.

"Dressed?" asked the intruder, a young woman in blue scrubs. She looked at Abby and nodded, walking into the room. "I'm Ruby, I'll be your ultrasound tech today. Are you ready to get started?"

Abby nodded and lay down on the table. Ruby spread a sheet over her lap and pulled up the hospital gown, revealing the swell of Abby's sweet belly.

My hands ached to rub over that bump. I took Abby's hand, needing to touch her in some way. She stiffened but didn't pull away.

"This will be cold," Ruby said before squirting some gel on Abby's stomach. "Do you want to know the gender?"

"Yes, please," Abby answered instantly.

"Okay," Ruby smiled. "I have to take some measurements and check the overall health, and then we'll look."

I sat with my eyes glued to the screen at the images of a tiny baby. My baby. I could see the head, spine, hands, feet. My heart swelled in my chest. It was the most profound experience of my life.

I glanced down at Abby as a single tear rolled down her cheek, a look of complete awe and joy on her face. My heart lurched into my throat. I intertwined my fingers with hers and gave her a squeeze. She squeezed back, hard. She glanced at me and gave me a little smile before returning her attention to the screen.

After several minutes, Ruby hummed thoughtfully.

"What?" Abby asked, looking between Ruby and the screen.

"Do you see that? Right there?" Ruby pointed to something on the screen. "That would be a penis."

"It's a boy?" Abby's grip tightened on my hand.

Ruby nodded and smiled widely. "Congratulations!"

"Thank you," Abby said quietly. I looked down at her. She looked radiant, glowing with joy, even as tears streamed down her cheeks. She wiped at them quickly.

"Thank you," I said to Ruby as she wiped the gel off Abby's stomach and lowered the hospital gown.

"My pleasure." She smiled and left the room.

"Did you want a girl?" I asked Abby.

"I've always wanted a daughter," she told me wistfully. "But I'll be happy with a son too. As long as he's healthy, that's all that matters."

I opened my mouth to tell her I'd be happy to try again, but she covered my mouth with her hand.

"Do not say whatever has you smirking like that," she said as she narrowed her eyes at me suspiciously. She lowered her hand slowly.

"You're no fun." I winked at her, and she blushed.

"I don't want to have to slap you in the doctor's office," she warned me.

"I don't think you would've slapped me," I teased her. "Maybe kicked me again or punched me."

She rolled her eyes again but blushed at the reminder.

"Can you step out so I can get dressed?" she asked.

"Do I have to?" I grinned wickedly.

"Yes." She gave me a glare, which was about as intimidating as a kitten, so I chucked her under the chin.

"Okay." I sighed dramatically. "I'll be right outside if you need help."

"I can put my own clothes on, thank you." She gave me a little push towards the door, but I resisted.

"One more thing," I said seriously.

Then I grinned and planted a kiss on her lips for the first time. She gasped in surprise at the electricity the mate bond elicited between us. I turned quickly and hurried out of the room before she decided to slap me after all.

I couldn't believe how much fun I was having with her. She was fun to tease and make blush. If she'd forgive me and get comfortable around me, it would be easy to see us hanging out all the time. I was suddenly hyper and excited, wanting to spend more time with her and get her to see that I'm not such a bad guy. Even if I did concoct and execute a plan that changed her life and hurt her.

A few minutes later, she walked out wearing her blue t-shirt, leggings and a pretty blush on her cheeks. I grinned at her, and she scowled, making me chuckle.

"Thank you for letting me be here," I said as I took her hand and led her out of the waiting room. I didn't know what it was that stopped her from pulling away from me but she didn't. I reveled in the small win.

"You're welcome," she said quietly.

"I'm all amped up," I admitted, bouncing a little with each step. "Let's go get something to eat, or buy out a baby store."

"Kade, no." She pulled her hand back, and I turned to look at her. There was a sadness on her face that broke my heart, reminding me of all the ways I hurt her.

"I'm glad you're excited, and I'm actually grateful that you were here with me, but I'm going back to work now." She looked away from me.

I turned and walked out of the doctor's office, not wanting to cause a scene. She walked out behind me, but we only got a few steps away from the door before I turned on her.

Abby

"Let me do something, Abby, please." His eyes begged me as he stared down at me.

My heart was absolutely aching in my chest. It was so unfair that I was so drawn to him and he was really quite charming. I hated that I still wanted him. I hated that I actually liked him. I wasn't ready.

"There's nothing left to do," I told him. "I already bought everything online."

"Let me take you out to eat," he suggested again.

"No." I shook my head adamantly. I had surprisingly enjoyed being with him today, but I wasn't ready for more.

"Are you ever going to forgive me?" he asked sadly.

My heart stuttered in my chest, emotions boiling to the surface. I wanted to run away, but my feet remained firmly planted on the sidewalk outside of the clinic.

"Sure. You're forgiven." I looked down at my stupid, leaden feet. "I'll see you around."

"You're a bad liar," he told me.

A tear escaped and rolled down my cheek.

He took a step closer and his voice came out pleading. "Please don't look so sad, baby. I can't take it. I'd rather you be angry and beat the shit out of me again."

A small giggle escaped me. I'd never live that down.

"Yell at me," he instructed. "Slap me, punch me, kick me. I can take it. But when you cry, I want to hold you so bad it hurts, and I know you don't want that."

More tears came, and I fought desperately to hold them in. He took a tentative step closer and put his arms around me. I stiffened.

"Please. Let me," he begged, and I lost it.

I bawled helplessly against his chest, and he tightened his hold on me.

I cried for myself. I cried for the way he hurt me. I cried for the cruel way he rejected me before he even knew me. I cried for my heartbreak. I cried for the way he said he needed me now, and my inability to forgive him. I cried for how sweet he was being, and how much I wanted him.

His arms were so strong, reassuring and comforting around me. I fit perfectly in his embrace and found myself calming down quickly.

"I want to tell you a story," he said into my hair as he held me close. "Can we just go for a drive or something? Please?"

"Sure," I agreed as I pulled away from him and wiped my face.

He opened the door to his pickup, and I climbed in as gracefully as I could in my condition.

He shut the door for me and ran around the hood. He drove in silence for a minute and then he started talking.

"My dad was thirty when he finally found his mate." He talked slowly as he navigated the streets. "She was only nineteen, young and beautiful, and human. She wanted nothing to do with him. His bear revolted, and he kidnapped her. She agreed to marry him and even gave him two sons."

His eyes darkened as he relived the story, he made a seemingly random turn, and I realized we were heading out of Ridgewood towards West Ridge.

"She always resented him though," he continued. "She hated that she never got to finish college, she hated living in West Ridge, she hated him for the life she had."

My heart hurt for him, and I put my hand on top of his, offering whatever comfort my touch would provide. He flipped his hand over and interlaced our fingers.

"She drank a lot. She slept around. She didn't take care of her kids. She hated us. And she rubbed it in his face. She told everyone about how she humiliated him and how pathetic he was."

He made another turn onto a gravel road. I looked around at the wooded area, wondering where he was taking me.

"Finally, she just left." He sighed and shook his head. "But the damage was done."

He pulled into a driveway, and I gasped as the charred remains of a house came into view beyond the trees.

"My dad was destroyed," he said quietly. "He burned the house to the ground and killed himself."

"Oh God." I squeezed his hand tightly and covered my mouth with my other hand. There was just a large pile of black rubble where the house used to be. The surrounding trees were damaged but healing now.

"It was nine years ago," he continued. "Kain had just turned eighteen."

"How old were you?" I asked.

"Eighteen." He shrugged at my confused look. "I'm only ten months older than him."

I nodded in understanding. "That's why you've always rejected the idea of a mate."

"Yes," he confirmed. He sighed deeply and stopped the car in front of the blackened remains of his childhood home.

"I was terrified," he admitted with a grimace. "I hated the fact that you would have enough power over me to destroy me. I hated knowing that you could hurt me so easily."

"And now?" I asked tentatively.

"I'm still terrified," he confessed. "But now I'm scared that I've ruined things before we even got a chance to try. I'm afraid you'll never forgive me."

"Kade–" I sighed, not even sure what I was about to say. I was overwhelmed and confused. It didn't make sense that I had such powerful feelings for him. I already felt more for him than I ever had for Simon.

I had to keep reminding myself that he'd done wrong by me. He'd hurt me worse than Simon had. He'd rejected me. He'd marked me. He'd made me pregnant without any thoughts of my feelings.

We sat in silence for a minute, and then he backed out of the driveway and drove us away from his sad memories.

"I saw you about a month before we met," he started talking again after he turned onto the gravel road. "At the home and garden show, do you remember?"

"I remember the show, sure." I furrowed my eyebrows. "But I'm sure I didn't meet you."

"No, we didn't meet." He grimaced and gave me a guilty look. "I asked someone who you were and then left. I went home and spent the next two days drunk out of my mind. Kain showed up and kicked my ass. The next day, I Googled you, and we had a private investigator look into you."

"Are you trying to piss me off again?" I scowled at him and crossed my arms over my chest, not liking that he'd completely invaded my privacy like that.

"No." He frowned as he glanced at me out of the corner of his eye. "I'm just telling you what happened."

He turned off the gravel road, and I sat quietly, waiting for him to continue.

"I judged you harshly based on your background check," he confessed with a grimace. "Between your parents, your recent breakup and your lack of friends, I was pretty sure you'd give the baby up for adoption."

"You skipped a few steps," I scoffed, choosing to ignore the judgmental words. "Like how you went from investigating me to deciding you wanted nothing to do with me to wanting to impregnate me at all."

"I didn't want a mate," he reminded me. He gulped and looked at me with guilt and shame. "I thought you'd be a massive bitch, and that I would be better off to just get you out of my system and move on."

"And the impregnating part?" I ground out, forcing myself to move on, in spite of the pain and anger.

"Well, I need an heir," he admitted sheepishly.

I punched his arm as hard as I could.

He didn't flinch. "I thought, if I had the cub, I'd be able to survive not having my mate."

I crossed my hands over my chest to keep from punching him again.

"And then?" I pushed him to continue. "When you realized that I would be keeping the baby and you couldn't adopt him?"

I realized I said *him* because it's a boy. I was having a boy! My heart sang again at the memory of Ruby telling us during the ultrasound, and I was momentarily distracted.

I looked around and realized Kade was slowly driving through a residential neighborhood. He made random turns and just drove.

"I thought about kidnapping the baby," he said, and I couldn't stop myself from punching his arm again. And again. I'd never felt such intense panic, and that was only from the threat of the possibility of someone kidnapping my baby.

"Are you fucking kidding me?" I screamed. I smacked his arm a few more times for good measure, making sure he felt my fury. "You bastard!"

"I said I thought about it," he reminded me with a sigh. "I wouldn't actually do it. Probably."

I scowled at him and crossed my arms over my chest again. "You're really not doing yourself any favors at this point."

"Yeah, well, I'm just trying to be honest." He frowned. "This is by far the longest conversation we've ever had."

"Fine," I huffed. "Go on then."

"Right," he cleared his throat. "Um, so, you were keeping the baby, and staying in Greenwood, and West Ridge. I was getting weaker, from marking you, and not being with you. Then Kain pointed out that West Ridge is a small town and asked what the hell I'd planned to do when I bumped into you randomly."

"At the hotel, I asked if you were from out of town," I pointed out.

"I didn't say yes," he reminded me. "I said it was a good

guess. It was a good guess, since I brought you to a hotel, but it was wrong."

I rolled my eyes at his intentional deception and me missing that detail.

"You planned the whole thing," I mused. "You already had the hotel room. You followed me to the bar. You planned to fuck me and knock me up."

He winced but didn't try to deny it.

"So why did you mark me if it weakens you?" I asked, still not understanding that part.

"It was an accident," he grimaced. "I got caught up in the moment."

I remembered the exact moment that he bit me, and I narrowed my eyes

"Why did you fuck my ass if you were trying to knock me up?" I demanded.

He shifted uncomfortably in his seat and bit his lip. I didn't think he was going to answer me, and I resigned myself to the fact that some guys just like anal.

"To make sure you were completely covered in my scent," he confessed finally. "So other bears wouldn't go near you."

"I smell like you?" I asked in alarm.

"Yes." A small smile played on the corner of his lips.

"Will I always smell like you?" I asked and discreetly smelled myself. "Does it go away?"

He growled, and I looked at him in surprise. His eyes were yellow. He pulled the truck over quickly and parked, taking deep breaths.

"Where are we?" I asked, looking around. I didn't recognize this neighborhood. I wasn't familiar with West Ridge yet.

"Just had to stop," he said through heavy breaths. "Kit's revolting."

"Who's Kit?" I watched him struggle with himself and knew the answer before he said it.

"My bear," he growled.

"He's upset that I was so alarmed about the smelly thing, right?"

He nodded, and I sighed.

"It's nothing against you," I told him. "It's not a normal human thing and it surprised me. I don't want to smell."

"You don't smell," he rolled his eyes as he got control of himself. "My scent is only perceptible by other bears… and wolves."

I held up my hand. "Bears are enough, let's not add wolves yet."

He chuckled, his eyes completely normal again.

"I have one more question about that night before we move on." I struggled to keep a serious face, and he gestured for me to continue. "Did you take a little blue pill?"

His head jerked back in surprise, and I almost laughed.

"Of course not!" he barked.

"Then how did you keep going like that?" I pushed.

He smiled wickedly, making my core clench. "I would've kept going if I hadn't marked you, causing you to pass out. I'm always hard when you're around."

My eyes darted down to his lap and his cock twitched against his pants. I forced myself to look back at his face, and he smirked at me. I rolled my eyes, desperately trying to keep my mind out of the gutter.

I reminded myself that he hurt me, I reminded myself that he rejected me.

I'll fuck you until you can't even remember his name. And the best part is, you won't even have to learn mine. I couldn't help comparing Kade to Simon. They were different in so many ways, except one, apparently.

"Great," I murmured to myself. "Just what I need, another oversexed…"

"Do *not* compare me to him," he snarled. He leaned

toward me until our noses were almost touching. "I am nothing like him. My cock will always be hard for you but *only* you, because you're my mate."

I nodded and gulped, turning away from his intensity. It was too much.

"If you've regained control of your bear, you can drive me back to my car now." I bit my lip and gestured for him to drive.

He put the truck back in gear and pulled away from the curb.

We sat, and stewed in our own thoughts for a few minutes before he started talking again.

"When do you expect to move into the house?"

"Three months," I replied automatically.

"You'll be, like, nine months pregnant." He frowned at me. "How are you going to be moving?"

"I'm not going to be moving," I rolled my eyes and then explained. "I'm going to be sitting with my feet up while the guys I hired move my stuff. The house will be finished and furnished. The movers will carry the few things I'm bringing from my apartment and bring the rest to charity. Then the movers will bring the baby stuff I have in my storage unit. Gus said he'd put together the crib and changing table for me."

"Who's Gus?" he growled.

"My contractor," I told him. "He's like a father to me. He has four kids, besides his building background. He could build a crib in his sleep."

"Did you tell your parents?" he asked softly, knowing it was a sore subject.

"Yes." I didn't offer more.

"Do you want to talk about it?" he pushed.

"Nothing to say." I shrugged with a nonchalance I didn't feel. It hurt that my parents were so disconnected and cold, but they'd always been like that so it was no surprise.

"My grandparents would've loved you," he changed the subject abruptly. "My dad's folks, that's who lived at Greenhope. They were amazing. They passed on about fifteen years ago now, thankfully before the mess with my parents."

"So you would visit them at the house?" I asked, enjoying the thought of him running through the big house with his little brother.

"Every chance we got." He smiled and nodded. "Some of my happiest childhood memories are at that house."

"What happened to it? It was a mess when I bought it."

"Dad used to go there to hide and get drunk. He was violent when he was drunk."

"Did he ever hit you or Kain?"

"No, not Mom either. He only drank alone at Greenhope. Never with us."

That seemed weird to me, didn't misery usually love company? Why would he want to be alone at his parents' house, to get drunk? And why had he torn the house apart in his anger? It didn't make any sense to me. I may not have had the best childhood, but I'd never do harm to my childhood home. Something wasn't adding up.

"Was it hard for you to give it up?" I asked, returning my attention to the conversation as I watched the houses and trees outside my car window. "Won't you want to live there with your family?"

The thought was like a knife to my heart, but just because I was pregnant with his son didn't mean he wouldn't go on to have a wife and kids.

"Baby, you're still not getting it." He frowned as he turned onto one of the busier main roads. "You're it for me. If you reject me, if you turn me away, then that's it. I'll never have another woman. I can't. I marked you, I sealed the bond. My bear won't allow it."

"No pressure," I mumbled.

"I'm not trying to pressure you, Abby," he said. "I'm just telling you how it is."

"You don't want a mate, but your bear insists on being with me," I summarized callously to test him. "He won't let you fuck any other woman, so it's me or nothing. That's really romantic."

"I'm not really a hearts and flowers kind of guy," he admitted with a grimace. "But I'll buy them for you if you like them."

"I don't want flowers!" I shrieked, pissed that out of everything I said, he was thinking about that.

"Ignore that last comment," he rushed out as he turned onto the road I recognized as leading back to the doctor's office. "What I should've said is, yes, my bear is possessive and insistent, but it's not just him. I like you. If I didn't I'd have an easier time staying away from you."

"Well, that's something, at least," I grumbled.

"Tell me you'll try to forgive me, or I'm going to keep driving forever," he threatened. "Better yet, let me take you on a date."

"Kade," I sighed. "I need time to think. I'll promise that I'll try to forgive you for the sake of you letting me out of the car, but that's all I can do for today."

"Well, that's something, at least," he mimicked me as he pulled to a stop next to my car.

"Please don't creep along the tree line tomorrow," I teased him before I got out. "You can come see the progress on the house instead, okay?"

His lips curved into a smile, and he nodded. He jumped out of the truck and gave me a helping hand down.

"One more thing," he said with a smirk and then kissed me quickly, causing my lips to tingle.

I pushed him away playfully.

"Control your bear," I scolded, secretly loving it.

"That was all me, baby." He winked. "Kit is the animalistic, possessive, me bear, you woman, mine, alpha type. He's not teasing or playful."

"I'll keep that in mind." I rolled my eyes and got into my car. He shut the door and waved as I drove off.

Chapter 8

September 2nd
Kade

She was probably going to kill me, but I couldn't resist. Her car was a piece of shit, and I didn't like seeing her driving it. I certainly didn't want to see my son riding in it.

I'd just finished relaying all my orders to Holly when Kain wandered into my office. I rolled my eyes. *Perfect timing.*

"You know most babies are fine with Target or Macy's or something," he joked immediately.

"Working hard again today, I see." I forced myself to look busy with the latest expense reports.

"Says the guy spending most of the morning baby shopping and sending our assistant out on personal errands," he threw back.

"What do you want, Kain?" I looked up and glared at him "If it's just to rub it in my face, then fine, you win. I was an asshole. I fucked up. She's not Mom. And yes, I want her now. Happy?"

"Ecstatic," he said jovially. "I hope she puts your balls through the wringer to make up for what you did to her."

"Dickhead," I muttered. "I remember you helping with the idiotic plan, you know. I can't wait until you meet your mate, and I get to watch you panic and fuck up."

"You love me." He grinned.

"I have no idea why."

"Because I'm your baby brother." He shrugged, then gave me a rare serious look. "All shit aside, it'll work out, right? She's going to forgive you, and let you see her and the baby?"

"She's going to let me see the baby," I informed him hesitantly. "And her. She understands everything. But she's still figuring out if she can forgive me."

"I think she will," he nodded once, resolutely. "She's got a good head on her shoulders."

"Thanks," I sighed. "It's a boy, if you haven't heard."

"I did," he said with a sheepish grin. "I guess I can call off my spies now that you're talking to her."

"Yes, you can." I scowled at him.

"I was just trying to help." He held up his hands defensively.

"I know," I admitted reluctantly. "And I'm grateful."

"So, what all did you put in the car?" he asked with a mocking grin. "I only heard about the clothes."

"Go back to work and stop gossiping like a teenage girl," I chastised him.

He laughed as he sauntered out of my office.

Abby

. . .

At almost exactly noon, I was thinking about taking a break for lunch when a shiny white Audi Q7 pulled up to the house. A middle-aged woman got out and waved at me happily. I waved back hesitantly, surprised and confused, as I approached her. Her hair was perfectly coiffed and her navy pant suit was impeccable, but she wore a wide smile and had kind eyes.

"Are you Abby?" she asked brightly.

I nodded.

"I knew it. You're gorgeous." She pulled me into a hug, and I was basically shocked to my core. She pulled back just as suddenly. "All right, sweetie. Here's the keys. I grabbed you lunch since I was coming. It's on the passenger seat, and everything else is in there."

"Who are you?" I asked finally.

"Holly." She gave me a questioning look. "Kade's assistant. Didn't he warn you that I was coming?"

I shook my head as I looked down at the Audi key she placed in my hand.

"What a shit!" She laughed. "Oh honey, I'm sorry. Be sure to give him an earful. He gave me very specific instructions to bring you this stuff. Do you have his number so you can call and yell at him?"

I nodded again.

"Great," she said with a big smile as a black Lincoln Town car pulled up behind the SUV. "That's my ride. I'm sure I'll be seeing you. Enjoy!"

She turned and walked to the car, getting in the back, before it turned and drove away.

I tentatively approached the SUV. It was obviously brand new, not a speck of dirt to be found. I opened the door slowly, half expecting Kade to jump out or something.

It was sparkling clean, a sleek gray interior, with the new car smell, mixed with whatever smelled so delicious in the to-go container sitting on the passenger seat. I peeked in the back, there was a blue car seat already installed and bags and bags of stuff.

"Huh," I grunted. I grabbed the to-go container, because it was making my mouth water, and shut the door. I sat on the front steps, dug into the amazing ravioli with a moan, and pulled out my phone.

I didn't want to talk while I was eating, so I texted Kade.

Abby: *Explain.*

Kade: *You need a new car. I bought you one. You're welcome.*

Abby: *Not okay, Kade Barrett!*

Kade: *Why not? What part do you protest to, specifically?*

Abby: *All of it! Except the ravioli, that's delicious.*

Kade: *Ironic since that's the only thing that wasn't specifically from me.*

I snorted a giggle around another delicious mouthful. It was so good, I loved pasta.

Kade: *You can't protest me buying clothes. It's my kid too.*

Abby: *I haven't looked in the bags yet. I only got as far as the car and the ravioli.*

Kade: *So the way to your heart is through your stomach?*

Abby: *I'm pregnant… I'm always hungry. And this is to die for.*

Kade: *Tell me you moan when you take a bite. Better yet, send me a sound clip.*

Abby: *No! And you're ridiculous. Have someone come get this car.*

Kade: *No. It's yours. Check the title, baby. It's in your name. If you don't like it, trade it in for one you do like.*

Abby: *It's not that I don't like it, Kade. It's a gorgeous car. But you can't buy me things like this.*

Kade: *Yes, I can.*

Abby: *No, you can't.*

Kade: *Yes, I can.*

Abby: *Are we just going to go back and forth?*

Kade: *If you want to. I like talking to you.*

Abby: *Kade, I can't keep this car. It's not right. I can buy my own car. I just haven't yet.*

Kade: *I saved you from having to go through the trouble. You can keep it. You will keep it, unless you don't like it. I'll buy ten more and parade them in front of your house, and you can pick the one you like best.*

Abby: *Do Not Do That!*

Kade: *Do you like it?*

Abby: *Yes.*

Kade: *Great. I'm glad. Is white okay? I thought black would be too hot.*

Abby: *You're impossible. White is fine.*

Kade: *What's your favorite color?*

Abby: *Blue, why?*

Kade: *Curious. What's your favorite ice cream?*

Abby: *Vanilla soft serve. Like, from Dairy Queen. So good.*

Kade: *Boring, yet specific. I like it. What's your favorite flower?*

Abby: *Roses, I guess. I haven't thought much about it. I've never gotten flowers before.*

Kade: *Are you just saying roses because they're the most popular then?*

Abby: *No. They're pretty. I like the way they start as a bud and then bloom. Like they're all tight and scared, but then they relax into something beautiful.*

Kade: *Very poetic. Have you looked in the car yet?*

Abby: *Just a peek in the backseat. The car seat is cute, looks designer.*

Kade: *It is designer.*

Abby: *Who buys a baby a designer car seat?*

Kade: *People who can afford to buy an Audi without blinking.*

Me: *So... you. Why do you drive a pickup if you can afford Audis?*

Kade: *I'm not a small man. The truck is comfortable. And it's good up in the mountains.*

Abby: *I finished lunch. Going to go investigate just how ridiculous you are.*

Kade: *Don't forget to look in the trunk...*

That piqued my curiosity instantly, and I pushed the trunk release button on the keys. It rose easily, and I walked around the car. I gasped as I took in the six heaping bouquets of roses. Dark red, pink, yellow, peach, purple and white with dyed blue tips.

I saw the cards peeking out of each and reached for the one in the white with blue tips bouquet. *"Because you're having my son."* Tears formed in my eyes.

I reached for the one in the red bouquet, *"Because I like you a lot."*

The pink bouquet, *"Because I want you."*

The peach bouquet, *"Because we need you."*

The purple bouquet, *"Because you're special."*

Tears were flowing down my face by the time I reached for the last card. The yellow bouquet said, *"Because I'm so sorry."*

Each bouquet had two dozen roses in it, and I giggled as I realized I had no idea what to do with all these flowers. For all of Simon's charm and charisma, he'd never once bought me flowers. Not even for Valentine's Day.

I couldn't believe Kade did this. He said he wasn't a hearts and flowers kind of guy, but he also said he'd try if that's what I wanted. My heart swelled as I wiped the tears off my face.

I really didn't care about the flowers themselves, but the entire gesture was the most romantic thing anyone had ever done for me.

I left the trunk open and looked in the back seat. There was a ton of baby boy clothes, all from Gucci and Versace. I rolled my eyes at the designer names, but couldn't help admiring how cute the clothes are. He was going to be the best dressed baby in West Ridge, for sure.

There was also a huge stack of diapers and a giant bag full of chocolate candy hearts—which I assumed were for me and not the baby. The last bag I came to had a black maternity nightgown and robe. I ran my fingers over the buttery soft material, which was going to feel like heaven against my skin. I sighed and closed the doors to the fancy SUV.

I sat back on the steps of the house and pondered the gifts.

"Looks like you got the weight of the world on your shoulders, girl." Gus sat next to me. "Care to share?"

"The father of my baby sent gifts." I gestured to the car. I wasn't used to sharing with other people, but I trusted Gus, and I felt like I needed to talk to someone. Normally that would have been Liam, but, well… he burned that bridge.

"It's not that asshole who cheated on you, is it?" Gus scowled. I didn't even know how he knew that.

"No, it's Kade Barrett," I admitted.

"Barrett?" He perked up at the name drop. "I've worked with them. Good kids. Shame about their dad."

I nodded sadly.

"At least you know he can afford the fancy wheels," he told me with a joking smile. "So what's the problem?"

"The problem is that he was a giant asshole to me," I explained vehemently. "He used me and rejected me. And now he decides he wants me, so he's sending me fancy gifts."

"I get it," he sighed. "Well, if you don't want him, tell him to take his fancy car and shove it."

I hesitated, and Gus noticed.

"Keep the car," he told me with a smug look. "It doesn't mean you've forgiven him. You need a nice car for you and your baby."

I stayed quiet as I pondered my options.

"Can I ask you a personal question?" he said hesitantly.

"Sure," I replied and shrugged. I didn't have anything left to hide.

"Are you his mate?"

My head snapped up, and I looked at him in surprise. "What do you know about it?"

"Girl, I've lived in West Ridge all my life." He smiled slyly. "I've known many bears. Including the old man. I've seen that bear sitting in the tree line almost every day since we got here. Didn't know it was Kade, but only one reason for him to be hanging around looking like a lovesick idiot. So?"

"Yes," I admitted. "That's what he tells me."

"Then he won't be able to stay away from you," he told me. "It goes against his nature. I'm sure, whatever he did, he's regretting it. It's probably causing him extreme pain, actually."

"He tells me that too," I agreed. "He never wanted a mate, because of what happened with his parents. He said he thought he could handle it, but didn't expect me to be... well, me."

"He was expecting a heartless bitch like his mother." He spit out the word *mother* like it gave him a bad taste in his mouth.

"Did you know her too?" I asked.

"Met her once," he said. "She was a piece of work. Basically propositioned me, if you know what I mean, right there, in front of her husband. Her eyes were dead. No heart. Total opposite of you."

"I'm kind of a bitch," I confessed.

"No," he denied with an adamant shake of his head. "You've been hurt, and you're cautious. You resist letting people get too close because you're afraid."

"How do you know that?" I wiped away the tear that escaped.

"Because I'm a wise old coot," he grinned. "And because I've seen it before. I wasn't sure about you at first, but I finally figured it out. You have a good heart, Abby."

"Thank you." I wiped away the flow of tears that wouldn't stop and forced out a giggle at how silly I was being. "Sorry for crying."

"We can blame the pregnancy hormones," he joked.

"Thanks." I sniffled. "And thanks for the advice."

"No sweat." He groaned as he stood up, and I chuckled at him. I'd seen him squat while carrying a huge stack of two by fours, so I knew he was just putting on a show.

I dropped my head into my hands when I was alone again. *Kade Barrett. What am I going to do with you?*

I knew what I wanted to do with him…

Chapter 9

September 2nd
Kade

She didn't text me back for the rest of the day, and I was getting nervous. She said I could stop by and see the house today, but I wanted to give her time to think if that's what she needed.

If I didn't hear from her by tomorrow, I'd leave work early to go see her. I'd just finished up for the day and walked down to my car when my phone beeped.

Abby: *Can you come by my apartment?*

Kade: *Everything okay?*

Abby: *Fine.*

Cryptic, but I wouldn't say no to any opportunity to see her. I sped across town to her apartment. I pulled up in front of her building, hopped out of my car and ran inside, unable to contain my excitement.

I hesitated just before I reached her door. What if she

wanted to tell me she couldn't accept the car? What if she told me to fuck off? What if she rejected me? Terror clawed at my chest as I approached her door. I forced myself to raise my hand and knock anyway. Whatever she had to say, I'd get through it. I'd talk her out of it, somehow.

I heard noise on the other side of the door, and then she opened it. She looked gorgeous in a simple white dress, hanging loosely over her curves and little belly, her bare feet peeking out beneath it.

"Come on in," she said with a soft smile.

I walked in and then burst out laughing at the amount of roses covering her apartment. They were literally everywhere. She'd separated them into multiple vases, dividing up the different colors.

"I had to buy vases," she told me. "Thank you, I love them."

"You're welcome." I returned my attention to her, my eyes greedily taking in every inch of exposed perfect skin, my bite mark on her graceful neck, the swell of her breasts beneath her dress.

"Have you eaten?" she asked me, a blush forming on her cheeks from my obvious gawking. "I just finished making stir fry. Would you like to join me?"

I nodded, not trusting my voice, barely believing she wasn't throwing me out and was actually inviting me to eat with her.

"How was your day?" she asked as she walked into the small kitchen.

"Fine," I replied automatically as I watched the gentle sway of her hips.

She pulled two plates down from the cupboard and the clinking noise snapped me out of my lustful haze.

"Do you need a hand?" I asked as I approached her.

"No, thanks." She gave me a bright smile over her

shoulder and my heart pounded wildly. She was so beautiful when she smiled. I wanted to see it every day.

"How was your day?" I asked, as she dished food onto the plates.

"Well, it was kind of crazy," she grinned mischievously. "Some lunatic bought me a car and sent me a ridiculous amount of roses."

"Lunatic?" I scoffed playfully.

"But I had an awesome lunch," she continued as if I hadn't spoken. "And we finished gutting the house, so we get to start on the fun stuff."

"We?" I jerked in alarm. "You better not be working alongside the construction workers."

"Of course not," she said with an amused look.

She set our plates at the table and sat down before I could help her with her chair. I shook my head at my own awkward hesitation. I was still nervous, and I didn't know what to make of this, and it was making me act like an idiot.

"I'll put up backsplash and paint, or other light work," she told me. "But I leave all the heavy stuff to the guys. Not that they would let me help anyway."

"Good," I grunted as I sat down next to her. The smell of the stir-fry hit me suddenly, and my mouth watered. I took a bite and groaned.

"Fuck, woman, you can cook, too?" I smiled as she giggled at me. I liked making her giggle.

"Don't get too excited," she said. "I only know how to make a few things. I taught myself how to cook, with the help of cooking shows and various books. I struggle with some things, like pasta. I can't seem to cook the noodles right. I don't know what it is. That's why I enjoyed the ravioli so much today."

"I can teach you how to cook pasta," I offered.

"You know how to cook?" she asked skeptically.

"Only a few things," I admitted. "Like you. But pasta is in my wheelhouse. I make wicked spaghetti and my lasagna is basically famous."

"Basically?" she asked with amusement.

"Yep," I joked. "The three people who have tasted it rave about it constantly."

She laughed and shook her head. A comfortable silence fell as we ate, and I was really enjoying just being near her, but I also wanted to know more. I wanted to know everything about her.

"Did you invite me over to talk about something?" I asked when I finished chewing the last bite.

"Not really," she said as she looked away from me. "I wanted you to see how crazy overboard the flowers are. And I wanted to thank you for the car and everything."

"You're welcome." I swiveled around to look at the roses covering her living room. "I think they're perfect. Not overboard at all."

"You're impossible," she said with amusement.

"So you keep saying." I turned back and smirked at her. "But the truth is, I'm quite easy."

She winced, and I understood immediately.

"For you, Abby." I reached out and took her hand. "I'm only easy for you."

"Sorry," she said softly. "That's a sore spot that's going to take a while to heal."

"I understand." I raised her hand to my lips and kissed the back. "I'll never cheat on you. I physically can't."

"I know you say things like that to reassure me, but it sounds weighted, like more pressure on me to be with you just because you don't have a choice in the matter," she confessed, looking down at her lap.

"I don't mean to," I assured her. "I'm really not trying to push or rush you. I didn't mean it like that. I should've just said I'd never cheat on you. I'm really not like that anyways. If I was a normal human guy, and I wanted out of a relationship or I wanted to fuck someone else, I'd have the balls to say it. And it certainly wouldn't be a dude."

She winced, but then nodded and gave me a weak smile.

"I appreciate you being understanding about my hesitation," she said softly. "I don't want to get hurt. I don't want to hurt you."

"I won't hurt you again, baby." I reached out and placed my hand against her cheek. "I've learned my lesson."

I stroked her smooth skin with my thumb, and then shifted my hand to brush against the corner of her mouth. Her lips parted instinctively, and it took all my strength not to lunge over the table and kiss her. She was too perfect, too beautiful. I wanted her with every fiber of my being, stronger even than the mate bond itself. I wanted to get to know her, and hold her, and make her feel good.

"I want to ask you a favor," she said hesitantly. I withdrew my hand and gestured for her to continue.

"I don't know if I'm ready to forgive you," she admitted slowly. "Because what you did to me was really shitty."

I grimaced. She wasn't wrong.

"And I don't know if I'm ready for anything between us," she continued. "I just got out of a bad relationship before you dropped this bomb in my lap. I'm sorry, I know that's not what you want to hear."

"Baby, don't apologize." I took her hand and stroked the inside of her wrist with my thumb. "I know I was a dick. I know I deserve your anger. Tell me the favor. What do you need?"

She took a deep breath and then blurted, "Will you fuck me?"

I sat stunned for at least a minute. That wasn't even close to what I was expecting.

"Are you serious?" I asked, once I put my tongue back into my mouth.

She nodded and bit her lip. I was out of my chair in a heartbeat. I scooped her up, and practically sprinted towards her bedroom.

"Kade!" she shrieked. "Put me down!"

I reached her bedroom, laid her on the bed, and really kissed her for the first time, pouring my heart and soul into my kiss, showing her exactly how much I needed her and wanted her. She responded after just a second of surprise and kissed me back just as passionately.

I groaned into her mouth and started pulling at our clothes. I needed to touch her, I needed to feel her, I needed to taste her. Lust and desperation overrode everything else. I heard fabric ripping but I didn't stop. I couldn't.

The feel of her precious little baby bump gave me pause as my heart swelled with love for the child within, and I remembered I needed to be a bit more careful.

I pulled back and removed the remaining pieces of her clothing, pressing soft kisses to her belly. She ran her fingers through my hair, and I looked up to see a look of reverence on her beautiful face.

I gave her a smile and then shifted lower. I cupped her swollen breasts with my hands and buried my face between her legs, not teasing her but giving her exactly what she needed. She cried out and her hips bucked wildly against my face.

She came within a couple of minutes.

"Fuck, Daddy, I need you, please!" She pulled at my hair, trying to get me to move up her body.

I placed one last kiss to her hot center and then stood up and pulled off the rest of my clothes quickly. Sliding between her legs, I was careful to keep my weight off her, and leaned down to kiss her lips as I entered her.

She wrapped her legs around me and moaned as I slid home.

"Fuck, baby, you feel so good," I groaned against her lips as I stroked into her.

"Oh, God, Kade," she gasped. "I forgot how big you are."

"You like my cock inside you?" I asked, increasing my pace as need gripped my spine. "You like the way I fuck you?"

"So much," she moaned out, clawing at my back to get me closer. "Don't stop."

"No chance of that," I told her, dropping down to my elbows while making sure I stayed off her stomach. "I never want to stop. I want to fuck you forever, baby. Every day, every night. Fuck, Abby, you're so beautiful."

As if pulled by an invisible force, I leaned down to kiss her again. I devoured her mouth, savoring her taste. I knew I'd never get enough.

When I felt her start to clench and shake around me, I could barely control myself. I turned my face to her neck and licked my mark, knowing it would be a powerful erogenous zone now.

"Kade! Fuck! Daddy!" she screamed as she came undone.

I roared out my release. I slowed down, but I didn't stop.

"Are you tired, baby?" I asked her. "Do you want me to stop?"

"No." She smiled softly. "Don't stop."

"Turn over for me." I pulled out and helped her roll over to her hands and knees before thrusting back into her wet heat.

"You're so hot, Abby," I said as I ran my hands over the swell of her hips and cupped the perfect globes of her ass. "I'm a lucky bastard."

I reached around and rubbed her clit while I fucked her hard from behind. I loved feeling her. I wasn't kidding when I said I never wanted to stop. I'd go all night if she didn't need sleep. I stroked into her for a long time, savoring every second, placing kisses on her back and neck until finally, she came again, and I followed.

Abby

Kade collapsed onto the bed next to me and pulled me against his chest. I felt better than I had in months, completely sated and comfortable. After a few minutes of us just catching our breath, the air became heavy and tense.

"Do you want me to stay or go?" Kade asked quietly.

Everything inside me wanted him to stay, but I couldn't do that yet. I asked him to fuck me because I'd been going out of my mind with lust since he showed up at my apartment two weeks ago. Plus, I wanted to see if he was really as good as I remembered.

He was better. He hadn't been as rough or domineering as he was at the hotel. His touch still lit me up in ways I didn't know were possible, and he had an unbelievable stamina.

"You should probably go," I forced out.

"Okay." His voice was casual, but I felt him tense against me. I felt bad for upsetting him, but I wasn't ready for him to stay. I wasn't ready to blindly give in to the mate bond. I still didn't quite trust it.

He got up, and I watched him pull on his clothes. He had ripped his shirt in his haste to get it off, and I giggled at the way it hung off him. He ripped my dress too, but I didn't care. I wrapped the sheet around my body and got up to walk him out.

"Can I come see the house tomorrow?" he asked as we walked to the door.

"Sure," I said with a shrug. "It's just studs right now, not much to see."

"Are you trying to talk me out of coming to see you?" he asked with a frown. "You know the house is just an excuse."

"I forgot," I admitted. "I'm not used to people wanting to see me."

"Better get used to it." He kissed my forehead and turned to open the door. "How about I bring lunch? How many guys are working? I'll bring a shit ton of pizza."

"There's like twenty, but you don't have to do that," I told him.

"I want to," he said, leaning against the open doorway. "What's your favorite topping?"

"Pepperoni," I said and then added the truth, "and pineapple."

"Fruit on pizza." He shook his head and grinned at me. His sexy grin made me want to pull him back into the bedroom.

"I know," I sighed. "I get a lot of shit about it. I usually just get pepperoni unless I'm alone."

"Never again," he ordered. "You get what you like."

"Yes, sir," I teased.

"It's yes, Daddy," he countered with a wicked smile.

"I'm never calling you *daddy* again," I threatened. "You told me to call you that because you were planning to knock me up."

He sighed deeply and sadness filled his eyes. I was mostly teasing, but it was also true. The seconds ticked by and then his sadness shifted back to a teasing glint.

"You called me Daddy in bed," he reminded me. "Just a little bit ago."

I blushed. I knew I did, but I hadn't been thinking clearly.

"Damn, you're cute when you blush," he told me. "I gotta

try to make you do that more often. That and laugh. You have a beautiful laugh."

I didn't know what to say to that. He's being so sweet but all I could think was, *where was this guy six months ago?*

"Thanks," I said quietly, falling into a weird mood. "I'll see you tomorrow then."

If he noticed my mood change, he didn't comment. He leaned in and gave me one last kiss before turning to leave. I shut and locked the door, leaning against it heavily.

I touched my hand to my swollen lips. Holy shit, the first time he'd really kissed me... *wow.* He'd given me two little pecks before that had shocked me like a jolt of electricity, but it was nothing like a real kiss. *That* was what Lisa had wanted to know about when she asked me about our kiss. I made a mental note to tell her next time I saw her. *That* was worth telling.

Chapter 10

September 3rd
Abby

"Special delivery for Abby," Gus yelled into the house cheerfully.

I glanced at the clock, it was already noon. Time went so quickly. All I'd done was some sweeping of debris, directed a few deliveries, talked to the landscaping crew and went over some details with Gus.

I hurried to the front door where Gus was standing next to Kade, who was hidden behind a massive stack of pizzas.

"Guys!" I yelled. "Pizza!"

Everyone appeared and started grabbing pizzas from the pile. Before I knew it, Kade and I were standing alone, and he was only holding one box. He handed it to me with a smile.

"This one's yours," he said.

A man appeared next to him, and I had to do a double take, they could have been twins.

"Did I miss anything?" the newcomer said. He stepped forward and extended his hand to me. "I'm Kain. The handsome, smarter and younger brother."

I laughed and shook his hand.

"Abby," I offered. "Thank you for suggesting to offer me the house. I love it."

"Ah!" He grinned widely. "Kade admitted that, did he? I figured he'd take the credit."

Kade elbowed his brother, who grunted, but they were both smiling.

"He admitted it," I told Kain. "Along with a few other things."

"I can only imagine," Kain joked as he eyed me appreciatively. "I hope you don't mind me crashing. I wanted to meet you, and see the house, of course. You're fucking adorable with your little belly. I hope my mate looks that cute pregnant."

"Um, thanks." I laughed. "I can see you're the strong, silent type."

"That's Kade," he replied honestly. "I'm an open book."

"She was being sarcastic, dumbass," Kade told him.

"I know that, dickhead." Kain rolled his eyes.

I shifted the pizza box in my hands as I watched them. Kain had a scar above his eyebrow, and his eyes were slightly greener, but otherwise they were pretty much identical.

I wondered if my son would look just like them, if so he was going to be a heartbreaker for sure.

"Do you mind if we look around while you eat?" Kade asked me.

"Not at all," I gestured into the house. "Go ahead. I'm going to sit outside and get some sunshine."

Right on cue, my stomach rumbled.

"Sorry," I said with a blush. "I'm always hungry these days."

Kain turned to Kade suddenly and yelled, "You're such an asshole!" then stomped off into the house.

"What did I do?" I asked in shock.

"Nothing," Kade assured me. "He's reminding me that I fucked up royally. He thinks you're adorable."

"Oh." I blushed more. "Okay."

"You are adorable," he said, dropping his voice lower and taking a step closer. "When you blush like that, I want to kiss you so bad."

I angled the pizza box so it was between us, blocking his advance. He was not going to get me all hot and crazy with my entire crew here to witness it!

"I'm going to go eat lunch," I told him with a smirk. "You go take your tour."

His eyes showed me his displeasure, but he maintained a neutral expression. I walked outside, sat on the front steps, and happily ate my pepperoni and pineapple pizza.

I put away three pieces before I started feeling guilty and bloated. I closed the box and breathed in the warm summer air. It was so peaceful and beautiful here, you'd never know it was actually right in town, the way it was surrounded by trees.

It was actually towards the edge of town, near the base of Eagle Ridge. I'd learned that during one of my voyeuristic drives around town.

I heard the guys talking and laughing inside, but I didn't go in to investigate. I really wasn't needed here. I should have been checking on my other properties more often, but this one had taken precedence.

"How was your pizza?" I turned to see the speaker, it took me a second, but I realized it was Kain.

"Delicious." I smiled warmly. "Did you get any?"

"Nah," he waved me off as he sat down beside me. "I ate already. Kade got those for you and your crew."

I struggled for something to talk to him about. I didn't know much about him and I'd never been good at small talk.

"I wanted to apologize to you," he said with a lowered voice.

"For what?" I asked tentatively.

"For my role in the asshole's plan," he sighed.

"Do I even want to know your role?" I raised an eyebrow, and he winced.

"Probably not," he admitted. "Actually, maybe it would be better if you hated me and not him."

"I don't hate him," I assured Kain quietly. "I was pissed and hurt. I'm still trying to figure out if I can forgive him, but I don't hate him."

"Good." He nodded.

"He told me about your parents," I confessed. "I'm sure it really scarred you both."

"Yeah." He looked away uncomfortably and ran his hand through his hair. "Let's just say that neither of us have been looking forward to dealing with mates."

"Dealing with..." I shook my head. "That's harsh, but I understand."

"Having a bear is like having another person inside of you," he told me. "An animalistic alpha who absolutely loses his mind for his mate. If the man can't get the mate, the bear freaks out, and the man goes crazy."

"What if the man never meets his mate?" I asked, now curious about how it all worked.

"Lucky him," he responded automatically, and then grimaced when he saw my shocked reaction. "How do I explain this? Like, now, I don't know my mate, so I can sleep with whoever I want. I could fall in love, get married, have kids, whatever. But if my bear meets his mate, it's all over."

"Does that happen a lot?" I asked. "A bear falling in love with a woman and then meeting another who's his mate?"

"No." He shook his head. "Very rarely. Most bears don't date until they meet their mates, it's just not worth it."

"But they still sleep around?" I pushed.

"Sometimes." He shrugged. "Lots of bears meet their mates when they're young. Although, you can't sense a mate until you're both eighteen."

"There you are." Kade appeared behind us and frowned at his brother. "I've been looking for you."

"He found me," Kain whispered conspiratorially, and I giggled.

"Please don't get chummy with him," Kade said to me. "He's a bad influence."

"I'm sure he would say the same about you," I remarked.

"Ha!" Kain barked out a laugh. "I knew I liked her."

Suddenly the radio inside was cranked up to full blast and Gus slammed the front door. We all startled, turning to see what got him so hot, but he looked guilty.

"What's up?" I asked first.

"Making sure nobody wants to follow me out here." Gus stuffed his hands in his pockets and looked from one brother to the other. "I want to tell you guys a story. It's really not my place, but I always thought it was fucked up, and you deserve to know."

There was a pause as we all stared at Gus.

"Don't keep us hanging!" Kain demanded.

"Maybe you better sit down, Kade." Gus gestured to the step next to Kain, and Kade sat robotically.

"All right, so you know your dad was already in his thirties when he met your mom." He glanced at me uncomfortably, and I gave him a reassuring nod, even though I had no idea where this was going.

"What you don't know is your mom died," he said with a sympathetic look.

Kade and Kain frowned and looked at each other.

"Your real mother's name was Kandace," Gus told the boys. "She died giving birth to Kain. Your dad met his mate, the woman you believed to be your mother about a year later."

He rubbed the back of his neck and watched them for their reaction as they sat in shock.

I couldn't imagine how they must be feeling, finding out their family story was all lies. I twisted my hands anxiously in my lap, worried about how Kade was feeling right now.

"That can't be true," Kain said finally.

"It explains why she never acted like a mother," Kade reasoned.

"She was resentful that your dad had a wife and kids before meeting her," Gus put in. "She made him go along with the story that you were her kids, because she hated the idea of your real mother."

"How do you know all of this?" I asked.

"I was just sixteen at the time, got my first job on a construction crew," Gus said. "We were supposed to be working here, on Greenhope, for your dad and mom. But when she died, he wouldn't set foot in the house, and our contract was cancelled. Your grandparents stayed in the house. Your dad felt bad for cancelling on us, so a year later, he hired us to build the new house for his new wife outside of town."

Suddenly I understood why their dad would come here to get drunk. It was supposed to be his happy home with the woman he loved.

"But…" Kain began, but couldn't finish the thought.

"If you don't believe me, Tessa Weking was the nurse on duty the night you were born," Gus said. "She's living at the senior living house now."

"Our mother wasn't really our mother," Kade breathed out.

I wanted to reach out to him, but Kain was sitting between us on the steps.

"I always thought it was bullshit, the way they hid it from you, especially after seeing the kind of woman Pauline was." He curled his lip in disgust and looked away. "When Abby told me you were afraid your mates would be like your mom, well, I decided that if I got the chance, I would tell you the truth."

"Why didn't Dad tell us?" Kain asked Kade.

Kade frowned as he considered it.

"I'm not saying I know what was in his head, and I don't know what it's like to be a bear with a mate," Gus spoke gently, "but I always figured, at first, your dad was probably relieved to meet his mate, and get a mother for his sons. He really loved Kandace, I could tell, but having a mate is special. Then, after Pauline left, he was destroyed. He'd lost the woman he loved, he lost his mate, and he lost his pride in the process. He probably couldn't tell you."

"What was Kandace like?" Kade asked suddenly.

"A lot like Abby, actually." Gus nodded at me.

Kain and Kade both turned to look at me. I gave them a weak, awkward smile.

"Smart, independent, caring." Gus considered it. "Reserved."

We sat quietly again, all lost in our own thoughts. I wondered how Kade was taking the news, and wished I was next to him to hold his hand. I also wondered how different he'd be if his mother hadn't died.

If his dad had met his mate when he was married to his mother, though, it would've created a whole mess of other problems for everyone. I sighed.

"Does she have any family?" Kade asked.

"I'm sorry, I don't know." Gus frowned.

"How could this be?" Kain snapped suddenly. "How could

we have lived our whole lives in this town and not heard it somewhere?"

"It's the best kept secret in town," Gus confirmed. "Your dad had half the town signing non-disclosure agreements. Myself included. But surely you've heard the one about the bear who got married and had kids before meeting his mate."

"There's no specific story, though," Kain insisted. "I always wondered what the hell happened. What happened to the first wife when the mate appeared?"

"Now you know," Gus said quietly.

"We have to go." Kade jumped off the steps suddenly.

Kain stood up slowly, and then turned and looked down at me with a wicked grin. "Bye." He leaned down and kissed my cheek.

"Kain!" Kade barked and pushed Kain away from me. "What the fuck?"

"Someone had to kiss the pretty girl goodbye," Kain said with a sly wink to me before challenging Kade. "Were you going to?"

Gus hid his grin behind a cough.

"Go wait in the car," Kade instructed Kain.

Kain gave me a little finger wave and sauntered off. Gus disappeared into the house.

"I'll see you later, okay?" Kade said when we were alone.

"Sure," I replied quietly.

He leaned down, kissed me softly on the lips, and then turned to leave.

I watched him get into the car and drive away.

Kade

. . .

"Did you know our father was married before he met our mother?" Kain challenged Holly as soon as we walked into the office.

She winced and guilty tears flooded her eyes.

"Let's go into my office," I suggested and led the way. Kain waited for Holly to follow me and shut the door behind us.

"Your dad made me sign an NDA!" Holly wailed as soon as the door was closed. "After he died, well, I didn't want to dig up old wounds. I'm so sorry, you guys!"

Tears flowed down her cheeks as she looked between us. I pulled her into a hug and rubbed her back.

"Did you know Kandace?" I asked gently.

"She was my best friend," she admitted. "I took this job to be near you, her boys. She loved you so much. She asked me to look out for you."

"She knew she would die?" Kain asked, surprised.

"No," Holly sniffed. "She thought your dad would meet his mate, and she'd be sent away. Her death was a total shock to everyone. Maybe a blessing though, she loved your dad, and his mate would've killed her. Maybe not literally, but it wouldn't have been pretty."

"Probably literally," I admitted.

Holly nodded and started crying against my chest again.

"Please don't fire me," she begged. "I really like taking care of you boys."

"We're not going to fire you," I assured her.

"We just want to know what you know," Kain put in.

We sat her down, and she started talking.

Chapter 11

September 3rd
Abby

Kade: *You still awake?*

Me: *Yes.*

Kade: *Knock, knock.*

There was a knock at the door. I pulled on my robe and went to let Kade in. He immediately pulled me into a hug.

"You okay?" I asked as I rubbed his back.

"Can I come in?" he asked, ignoring my question.

I pulled him in and locked the door behind him. He took my hand and led me to bed, laying me down, and crawling in behind me, spooning me.

"Do you want to talk about it?" I asked.

"No," he replied instantly.

"Um, Kade?" I shifted against his erection poking me in the butt.

"Ignore it," he huffed.

We lay in silence for a long time after that, and I thought he'd fallen asleep, but then he whispered into the darkness. "Please don't leave me, Abby."

My heart broke for him, for Kain, for his dad. I rolled over in his arms and held him close to me. His thick arms banded around me like a steel cage.

I didn't know if he was thinking about his mom dying during childbirth or the woman he thought was his mother leaving him, so I remained quiet and just held him. I eventually fell asleep, tangled up with him.

September 4th

Abby

I reached for Kade, but quickly realized I was alone and the other side of the bed was cold. I wondered when he left. I reached for my phone and saw it was already almost noon. My alarm hadn't gone off.

I texted Gus immediately.

Abby: *Late start this morning, be in soon.*

Gus: *Kade called me, said you were going to kill him for turning off your alarm, but you needed rest. Don't worry about us. Why don't you take a day for yourself?*

Me: *And do what?*

Gus: *Pack your apartment? Get a manicure? Read a book?*

Me: *I'll be there in a while.*

Gus: *You're pathetic. Workaholic.*

Me: *When's the last time you took a day off to get a manicure, Pot?*

Gus: *I took a day off and went fishing last year, Kettle.*

Me: *You took your entire crew.*

Gus: *Not fair if I get a day off and they don't. Speaking of, gotta get back to work. I don't want to see you today.*

I snarled in frustration. I couldn't believe Kade shut off my alarm and called Gus. But I could believe Gus didn't want me at the house today. He was always telling me to take a day off and stop breathing down his neck.

I was just getting ready for bed when I heard a knock at the door. I sighed, knowing who it must be. A quick look out the peephole confirmed it, and I opened the door for Kade. He entered, turned, closed and locked the door and then led me into my bedroom.

We lay down, and he wrapped his body around me without a word. I sighed in frustration, even as my body relaxed in the comfort of his arms.

"Are you okay?" I asked quietly.

He didn't respond.

"Kade?"

Silence.

"Daddy?" I tried.

"Don't call me that!" he barked, startling me.

"Oh, Kade." I tried to turn in his arms but he held me firmly. "I forgive you."

"You shouldn't," he whispered. "I was an asshole."

"Yes, you were," I conceded. "But you were scared, and I can understand that. The most important thing is you're nice to me now. And I can't be mad at you for getting me pregnant when I already love our baby so much."

"Hmmm." He let out a noise somewhere between a purr and a growl. "That makes me happy."

"Which part?" I asked.

"About our baby." He rubbed his hand over my stomach.

"I was thinking about it," I told him. "I was wondering if our son is going to look just like you and Kain. I can't believe how identical you two are."

"We look exactly like our dad did at our age. I remember seeing old pictures, but everything was lost in the fire."

"Do you think it would have made a difference?" I asked into the dark room. "If you'd known the story a year ago, would it have changed anything? It's still a terrible story."

"It is," he confirmed. "But there's one part that's significantly different."

"What's that?" I asked him.

"I had a mother who loved me." His hand rubbed my belly rhythmically as he talked. "She always knew my dad could meet his mate at any time, but risked it anyway. She asked her friends to look out for us if she got sent away after Dad met his mate. She named us after her to give us a piece of her that nobody could take away."

"What's your dad's name?" I asked, having never heard it.

"Grant," he answered simply. "I asked him once how we got our names. Our mother… or stepmom, I guess, her name was Pauline. Our names are just so unique. He said it was just a whim and changed the subject."

"What else did you find out about Kandace?" I pushed.

"Her parents died when she was young," he said. "She had no other family. She was in foster care until she aged out, then she lived with her best friend until she finished school. She worked as a waitress. That's how she met my dad. He started going to her restaurant every week to see her, until she agreed to go out with him."

"You must've found someone close to her," I mused.

"Turns out I've known her best friend my entire life," he said softly. "It's Holly."

"Your assistant?" I gasped.

I felt him nod behind me.

"She stayed close to you even though she couldn't tell you the truth," I said.

He nodded again.

My phone beeped on the nightstand, but I ignored it. I had no idea who it would be, but I didn't care.

It beeped again. Kade reached out and grabbed it. I heard his breath coming out harsher before he jumped out of bed, threw my phone down on the bed and stormed out.

"Kade?" I scrambled off the bed and followed him.

"Say it to my face, Abby!" he roared as he wheeled on me and pinned me with his intense gaze. "If you can't forgive me, if you hate me, if you don't want me, fine! I'll figure it out without you, but say it to my fucking face!"

"What are you talking about?" I took a step back, surprised by his anger and confused by his words.

"It's so fucking easy to string me along and punish me for hurting you, isn't it?" he yelled. "Get a paternity test!"

I was stunned speechless, and just gawked at him as he spun on his heel and marched out, slamming the door.

After a minute, I remembered my phone and ran back to the bedroom to see what the fuck he saw.

Simon: *Hey beautiful, it was good to see you. I need to see you again soon. I can't stop thinking about you and the baby. I'll see you soon. I love you.*

Oh fuck! What the fuck was Simon thinking? I told him the baby wasn't his! Kade had nearly killed him.

I ignored it for now and started typing out a text to Kade. Then I stopped myself. He didn't even ask for an explanation, he obviously didn't trust me. He had his own demons to deal with, and I had mine. Maybe it was for the best if I left him alone.

I texted Simon instead.

Me: *The baby is not yours. I'm one hundred percent positive. Do not text me again. Do not call. Do not come around. It will not end well for you. We are over. Forever. Goodbye.*

The next day, I woke up early, called Gus with instructions and then packed a bag. I got on the first flight out of town. I'd never done anything like that before, but I needed distance, I needed clarity, I needed a break.

Chapter 12

September 18th
Abby

I'd been gone for almost two weeks. I was sad and lonely, I missed Kade, as ridiculous as that was since I never even really had him. He hadn't texted or called, but neither had I.

I rented a little room at a bed and breakfast in San Diego, and marveled at my luck at getting somewhere so warm and beautiful for my mystery destination. I walked around Old Town, Seaport Village, Little Italy and the Gaslamp Quarter, toured Coronado, spent two days at the zoo, another at SeaWorld and just breathed.

I got a smoothie in Balboa Park, found a shady spot under a tree and opened my book, my third shifter romance since leaving. It was the first thing Lisa had asked me, so I figured maybe it would have some insight. So far, they just make me sad.

A large shadow fell over me, and I looked up at his face, seeing the scar immediately.

"How did you find me?" I demanded.

"Traced your credit cards," Kain admitted unapologetically.

"Are you here to apologize on his behalf, or to see if I'm flouncing around with another man?" I put my book aside and glared at him.

"I came to get your side of the story," he told me, holding his arms out in a 'let's have it' gesture.

"It's none of your business," I snapped.

"True," he admitted and stuffed his hands in his pockets. "Is there any chance the baby's not Kade's?"

"No!" I shrieked without thought. "Dammit. I said it's none of your business. Go away, Kain."

"Are you still fucking your ex?" he pushed, ignoring me.

"What will it take to make you go away?" I huffed.

"Tell me the truth." He put his hands out to his sides again.

"No," I snarled. "I haven't been with Simon since before I caught him fucking Liam. Two months before I met Kade. I saw him, once, at my apartment. Kade was there. Kade spoke to him more than I did. Simon texted me out of the blue, Kade read it."

I pulled up the text thread on my phone and threw it at Kain. He caught it easily.

"See for yourself," I snapped. "I didn't text him before. I told him the baby wasn't his and not to contact me again."

He glanced at my phone and handed it back to me.

"Come back with me, Abby." He held out his hand for me.

I scoffed. "You can leave now. You have my side. So, just… go."

"Abby, listen, Kade is miserable," he said quietly.

"That's his fault," I huffed. "He did all of this!"

"Did he?" he asked me. "He didn't send that text. Did you tell him that it wasn't what it looked like? Did you try to talk to him after?"

"He didn't ask!" I shrieked, startling a couple as they walked by. I lowered my voice and leveled Kain with a dirty look. "I didn't know what the text said when he freaked out, yelling at me for punishing him and demanding I get a paternity test."

Kain winced.

"He didn't ask if there was a chance the baby wasn't his," I continued. "I told him I forgave him. I guess he doesn't believe me."

I wiped furiously at the tears suddenly streaming down my cheeks. Fucking hormones.

"When are you coming home?" he asked.

"When I'm ready," I told him. The truth was, I needed to go back by the end of the week. I had a doctor's appointment coming up.

He turned to leave, and I stopped him. "Were you expecting to find me here with Simon?"

"No," he said with a little teasing grin. "But I hadn't expected to find you reading bad shifter romance novels either."

"This one's actually pretty good," I said, defending my book, holding it up so he could see the cover. "Mia Smith seems to know a lot about bears."

"Please talk to Kade," he sighed. "I didn't tell him I was coming. He doesn't know where you are, yet, but he's going fucking crazy."

"Literally?" I asked, really worried about Kade's mental health.

Kain gave me a look and then walked away.

Dammit. I picked up my phone and sent Kade a text.

Abby: *Fuck you for doubting that the baby is yours! You can be mad all you want. I won't ask forgiveness for something I didn't do. I'm in San Diego. I'll be home this weekend.*

He replied immediately.

Kade: *Fuck you, Abigail Bradley. I never doubted it, I can smell it. I didn't know if you knew it.*

Abby: *Fuck you, Kade Barrett! How could you think I'd still be seeing that piece of shit after he fucked my best friend?*

Kade: *Fuck you, Abby. He said he'd seen you.*

Abby: *Fuck you! You were there! That one time at my apartment. I didn't even open the fucking door to him until you got there and started choking him.*

Kade: *Fuck you. How was I supposed to know that's all he meant?*

Abby: *Fuck you, you could've asked.*

Kade: *I'm an irrational, jealous asshole.*

Abby: *I'm a hard-headed, stubborn bitch.*

Kade: *You're perfect.*

Abby: *Only a bear who thinks I'm his mate would think so.*

Kade: *Only the opinion of the bear who knows you're his mate matters.*

Abby: *Okay, then. Glad we talked. I'll see you next week.*

Kade: *I can't wait that long. Ready to rip my skin off. Come home sooner. Now, preferably.*

Abby: *I'm enjoying my vacation.*

Kade: *Fine.*

Abby: *I'm sorry you jumped to conclusions and thought the worst of me.*

Kade: *I'm sorry too, baby.*

I sent him a picture of my toes and the picturesque gardens in the background. He didn't reply. That was all right though, I already felt better, lighter, happier. I didn't know what was ahead, but it was a lot brighter than it seemed an hour ago.

I sat and read my book, took a long walk through town and stopped at a little restaurant in the Gaslamp Quarter. It looked like a local joint, and I figured it must be good since it was bustling.

I was seated in a small table across from a young couple with an infant son. They smothered him with love and attention, while giving each other adoring gazes, and it made my heart ache. I wanted that for my son. A happy home with a mom and dad who loved each other.

After I finished eating, I walked around aimlessly for a while, just enjoying the sights and smells of the city, and then I took a cab back to the bed and breakfast.

When I walked into the house, I froze. Kade was sitting on the couch.

The homeowner, Mrs. Thomas, sat in a chair adjacent to him, looking fairly uncomfortable.

Kade stood as soon as he saw me and gestured outside. I turned back around and walked outside with him behind me. I sat on the little front porch swing. He perched against the rail, watching me.

"What are you doing here?" I asked finally.

"I told you I couldn't wait until next week to see you," he said sheepishly.

"I didn't realize that meant you were going to jump on the next plane to come out here." I chuckled at how adorable he was when he was embarrassed.

"You look beautiful," he told me.

"You look like shit," I replied.

He had dark circles under his eyes, he looked like he'd lost weight, his hair was standing up everywhere and his clothes were wrinkled, but he was still handsome.

"I love you," he said with a grin.

I gaped up at him. "You… what?"

"I love you, Abby," he repeated. "Not Kit, the bear. Me,

the man. And not because you're my mate, but because you're blunt and stubborn and defensive."

"None of those are good qualities," I pointed out.

"Maybe, but I still love you." He took a step forward and held out his hand. I took it hesitantly, and he pulled me off the swing.

"You're the most beautiful woman I've ever seen," he said as he wrapped his arms around my waist. "I especially love you like this, pregnant with my cub. I want to keep you pregnant forever."

I slapped his chest, even though I couldn't hide the grin, and then I wrapped my arms around his neck.

"I love your feisty spirit," he continued with a smirk. "You're a fighter. I love that you worked hard to become your own person after having asshole parents. I love that you don't let people walk all over you. I love that you're not afraid to stand up to me."

"I get it." I raised up on my tiptoes and pressed a kiss to his lips. "You love me. I don't know that I'm there yet, but I know I want to be with you. I know I feel something really strong for you, and I know I've missed you like crazy."

"I'll take it, for now." He grinned and kissed me thoroughly. Our bodies molded together as he awakened all the emotions and desires that burned only for him. I rubbed against him shamelessly. He was here, he loved me, and he was mine.

He nipped my lower lip before he pulled back. "Go pack your stuff, baby."

"Kade! No!" I smacked his chest again. "I'm finishing my vacation."

"*We're* finishing your vacation," he told me with a smug grin. "At the Marriott. I don't think Mrs. Thomas would appreciate listening to the way I make you scream all night."

Oh!

I blushed deeply and turned away from him before he could tease me about it, beelining into the house to pack my bag. I heard him chuckle behind me, but he didn't comment.

Kade

I understood my dad a little better after those two weeks away from her. I was ready to apologize, beg her forgiveness, and even suffer through the humiliation of her sleeping around if it meant seeing her again.

Okay, maybe not the last one. I would've killed any man who touched her. She was mine.

After my initial jealous rage wore down, the more I thought about it, the less I believed it to be true. She just wasn't the type, I didn't even know how I knew that. I'd never smelled a man on her, though. And I really could smell my cub.

It was weird. I'd never heard of such a thing before, but I could smell me… on him… in her. I'd noticed it the first night she'd let me sleep in her bed. When I'd been too upset to say much of anything and held her like she was my lifeline.

Even after I doubted her continued relationship with her ex, I still needed to hear her say it. So I'd waited, miserable and restless.

Kit had been torturing me painfully, and I'll never know how I survived. I couldn't eat, I barely slept, and I spent every free second outside her house. I knew she'd come back one day.

I realized I loved her as soon as I opened her first text. I'd never felt such relief as when I read the second. I was already in a cab on the way to the airport by her third text. I was either getting on a plane or waiting there for her to get off one.

She emerged from the B&B suddenly. She absolutely glowed in her red and white sundress. I took her bag from her and put it in the backseat of my rental before helping her into the car. Once I was seated and we'd both buckled, I immediately reached over and took her hand.

"I suppose you've already seen the whole city?" I asked her as I pulled away from the curb.

"I wouldn't mind seeing it again," she answered with a soft smile.

"What was your favorite thing?" I asked.

"I don't know," she sighed. "Just walking around and exploring."

"Why the sigh?" I frowned as I tried to gauge her reaction while navigating the busy streets. I took the exit to the interstate toward downtown.

"How do you know where you're going?" she asked, looking around us.

"I have an excellent sense of direction," I told her.

"Is that a bear thing?" she asked.

"Only when I'm finding my way through the woods following a scent," I replied with amusement. "I've been to San Diego a few times. I love it here."

"Oh," she huffed.

"Are you disappointed that I'm not smelling my way back to the bayfront?" I teased.

"Of course not." She turned away to hide her blush.

I smiled but didn't push her for a confession. We sat in comfortable silence as I drove, and then I realized she'd fallen asleep next to me.

I pulled up to the Marriott, jumped out and tossed my keys to the valet. Then, I scooped her out of the passenger seat and carried her inside. She jostled but didn't wake up.

I carried her upstairs and tucked her into bed, immediately crawling in beside her and molding myself against her. We were both still dressed, but I didn't care about anything except feeling her against me, breathing in her sweet scent.

I'd already fucked up, after promising never to hurt her again. I had to be better for her, I couldn't risk losing her.

Chapter 13

September 19th
Kade

I woke up before her and slipped out of bed to get us coffee and the newspaper from downstairs. As I was getting off the elevator on our floor with my arms full, Kain almost barreled into me. I wasn't even surprised to see him there.

"Fuck, where's the fire?" I chuckled.

"No time, talk later." He rushed onto the elevator and hit the button repeatedly until the doors closed.

His hair was sticking up in every direction and his clothes looked disheveled. I'd never seen my brother look so frazzled, and I knew there was only one thing that could make him look like that… his mate.

I sighed deeply as I inserted the card into the door and pushed it open. Then, I smiled when I saw Abby's sexy body sprawled across the bed, her arm extended like she was looking for me in her sleep.

She was beautiful, so perfect. My heart ached at the sight of her, I was totally in love with her. Even if she wasn't my mate, I'd always want her by my side. I was addicted to her, her smiles, her laugh, what she said, how she moved, I couldn't get enough.

"Morning, baby." I set the coffee down on the nightstand and rubbed her back.

"Caffeine is bad for the baby," she murmured.

"I know, that's why I got you decaf," I bluffed.

"You did not!" She gasped and sat up quickly. "I can't function without one cup of coffee!"

"I was lying," I admitted. "I didn't know how serious you were about it."

"Jeez." She held her hand to her chest. "I panicked there for a minute, thinking you were going to deny me."

"I'll never deny you," I growled, raking my eyes down her tempting body.

"Don't start," she said playfully as she jumped out of bed and snagged her coffee. "There's no time for that now, we have things to do."

"Like what?" I sipped my coffee, amused by her apparent willingness to deny me.

She danced towards her suitcase, taking a swig of coffee, and then setting it down on the table before rifling through her clothes.

"There are hundreds of places to see in San Diego, Kade." She pulled out an outfit and then started undressing.

I groaned at the sight, first she was going to deny me and then she was going to torture me? Was this what married life was like? My lips quirked in amusement, that might not be so bad.

"Do you want to get married?" I asked on a whim.

"What?" she shrieked and spun towards me.

Unfortunately, she'd just finished removing her shirt, and her perfect breasts were bare and staring me in the face, so I completely forgot what I'd been thinking about. I moved towards them reflexively, but she jumped away from me and covered herself with her hands.

"Kade!" she squealed and fled as I moved to grab her. "No! Bad!"

"Good," I insisted, ignoring the part where she was speaking to me like I was a dog.

"Stay," she pointed to the ground at my feet and struggled to get her bra on without revealing herself to me.

"How can I stay here when your boobs are over there?" I teased, and she laughed.

She managed to get her bra on somehow, and then her phone rang, successfully ending our game.

I left her alone and went into the bathroom to shave and wash up. I was only halfway done shaving when she pounded on the door.

"Kade Barrett!"

Oh fuck. What had I done this time?

"I'm shaving. You can come in if you need to yell at me." I swiped the razor down the line of my jaw and waited for the firing squad.

The door crashed open and she stormed inside. "Do you know who that was? Do you know what they said? I can't believe you! You're ridiculous!"

"Baby, you're going to have to be more specific." I tried not to smile, but she looked so cute with her hands on her hips and her eyes full of indignation.

"You paid off the mortgage on my house!" she accused.

Ah. I hadn't expected her to find out about that yet.

"So?" I pretended to be ignorant in why my independent

little firecracker would be mad about that as I ran the razor down my cheek.

"You can't do things like that," she informed me.

"Yes, I can." I finished the last bit and wiped my face off.

"No, you can't."

"Yes, I can." I applied aftershave to my cheeks and grinned at her. She was even fun to argue with.

"I can buy my own house." She spun on her heel and marched out of the bathroom.

I caught up to her in two steps and wrapped my arms around her waist, nuzzling my nose into her neck. She smelled like strawberries.

I wanted to tell her that I damn well could pay for *my* house for *my* mate and *my* child, but I wasn't a complete moron.

"Don't be mad at me, baby," I begged instead. "Let's enjoy our vacation. Have you been to Embarcadero yet?"

"No," she sighed and her body relaxed in my arms. "I'm going to yell at you about it more later."

"Great." I released her and swatted her on the ass. "Finish getting ready. You can make a list while we're here, and yell at me about everything that makes you mad after we get home."

She gave me an amused look over her shoulder as she picked up her shorts. I shrugged. I didn't care if she yelled at me, as long as she didn't leave me again.

Abby

I hadn't realized that Seaport village was in Embarcadero when Kade asked me if I'd been there. I guess I had, but that was okay. I didn't mind seeing it again, and it all looked different with Kade by my side anyway.

Everything was brighter and more cheerful somehow. The sun was sunnier, the ocean was bluer, the people were friendlier, and I couldn't stop smiling like an idiot.

I'd been annoyed when my banker had called this morning and said that 'someone' had paid off the full amount on my mortgage, but after I'd gotten over my initial defensive reaction, I wasn't surprised or angry. That was just Kade.

Technically, it was his family house that he was giving to his son, and now that he wasn't hiding his identity from me, he'd gone ahead and cut out the middleman. It was actually kind of sweet, but it seemed like a waste of money. If he had just done things right initially…

No, I would not go down that line of thinking right now. As we walked through Waterfront Park holding hands, the last thing I wanted to think about was the pain he'd caused me.

It didn't take me long to realize that Kade was very tactile. If he wasn't holding my hand, he had his arm around my waist, or his hand on the small of my back. Even when we had lunch at a chic eatery, he barely stopped touching me long enough to eat. I didn't know if that was a bear thing or a Kade thing, but I liked it.

He made me feel cherished in a way I never had before. He listened when I talked, he talked when I showed interest in something, and if I even looked at an item in a shop, he had his wallet out. That was equal parts annoying and charming.

I hadn't meant to buy every bauble, souvenir and piece of jewelry I'd admired, and even if I had, I could have paid for it myself. At the same time, it was sweet that he was so perceptive and wanted to take care of me.

We had supper at a fancy restaurant in downtown San Diego, and then I let Kade take me back to the hotel early, and showed him how much I appreciated everything he'd done that day.

We didn't rush, we didn't rip each other's clothes off, we made love slowly and reverently. We cuddled and we talked, and it was amazing.

I let myself forget about everything for the first time in forever. Nothing else existed, and nothing else mattered.

September 20th

Abby

The next day, Kade booked us on a harbor cruise in the morning, we had lunch in Little Italy, and then we drove up to La Jolla to see Birch Aquarium in the afternoon.

After we left the aquarium, Kade held my hand as he drove the rental car through the fancy La Jolla neighborhoods.

"I want to buy you something," Kade said suddenly as I gazed out the window at a particularly spectacular luxury home.

"You've already bought me tons of stuff." I laughed.

"No, I mean something specific, something special." He stroked his thumb over the back of my hand as he smoothly navigated the winding roads.

"What?" I asked cautiously. He'd already bought me a car, and a house, not to mention the tons of souvenirs.

"A ring." He gave me a nervous look, and my heart melted a little, even though I was slightly panicked.

"What kind of ring?" I asked for clarification, just to make sure I knew what he was suggesting.

"Abby, I love you," he sighed. "I want to buy wedding rings and fly to Las Vegas right now, but if you want a big wedding, we can get you an engagement ring for now and start planning when we get home."

When I remained silent, he grimaced. "If you need more time, we can get a promise ring instead, but I'd really like to put a ring on your finger, if you'll let me."

I held my hand up to stop him from suggesting anything else. "Give me a minute to think."

He nodded and stroked his thumb over my hand while he drove us back to the hotel. I stared out the window, but I didn't see anything beyond the glass. My mind was suddenly too overwhelmed to enjoy the picturesque views.

Despite our rocky beginnings, Kade had quickly become my favorite person, but maybe that wasn't saying much since I didn't have too many people.

He respected me, which was really important to me. He was sweet and easy to be around, he made me feel alive and special. Was that love?

Kade said he loved me. I was his mate, which meant he'd never be able to let me go, not that I wanted him to at that point. The two weeks without him had taught me that I'm just as addicted to him, it had been sheer torture not texting him or calling him.

Even though I'd enjoyed my time in San Diego, I'd felt incredibly alone and broken, like I was missing a piece of myself. Was that the mate bond? I had no idea. I couldn't separate it all in my mind.

Maybe it didn't need to be separated, though. We were mates, we belonged together. He loved me and I loved him.

I loved him. Of course I did. How could I not? I wouldn't get so angry with him if I didn't. I wouldn't yell if I didn't care. I wouldn't be here if I didn't want to be. I'd never been the kind of girl to go along with niceties or play a role.

Kade parked in front of the hotel and waved the valet away from my door, offering me his own hand.

I let him help me to my feet, and then I put my hand on his arm to stop him from leading me into the hotel. He stopped and looked at me curiously, and I smiled as I said the words that would change our lives.

"I've never been to Vegas."

Chapter 14

September 24th
Kade

After the initial shock of her response, I'd swept her up into my arms and spun her around until she got dizzy. I'd wanted to leave for Vegas immediately, but she talked me into going up to the room for our luggage. Then, we landed in bed and stayed there until morning.

I booked us seats on the first flight to Vegas the next day, and we'd had just enough time to go to the jewelry store to pick out rings. I can't fucking believe she agreed to marry me! I must be the luckiest asshole on the planet.

I didn't even want to come home today, but Abby said she needed to get back for a doctor's appointment. Once we got back to Ridgewood, I realized we hadn't exactly thought things through or discussed anything.

I didn't know if I was supposed to invite her to my apartment, or if I was supposed to go to her apartment. The renovations on the house were still two or three months from completion, and I wasn't waiting that long to be with her permanently, but moving all of our stuff now, just to move again in a few months, seemed silly.

I had my driver take us to my apartment, figuring with her suitcase, she'd have anything she needed. I carried her over the threshold, and then, I made love to her well into the night. I'd never get enough of her.

I couldn't believe how happy she made me. I was still slightly terrified of it all going to hell one day, but she was so easy to be with and so incredibly easy to love.

Sept 25th

Kade

The next day, I joined her at the doctor in the morning, and then kissed her goodbye so she could go to work. I had half a mind to follow her around all day like a puppy, but decided to go to the office and get some work done instead.

"Look who decided to come to work," Kain snarled as soon as I walked in the door.

Since Kain was always good natured and easy going, it stopped me cold. "What happened?"

"Nothing," he barked.

"He found and lost his mate," Holly explained sympathetically.

"I got married," I announced. Probably the most inappropriate moment ever, but I couldn't keep it in anymore.

"Good, a late bachelor party is a good enough reason to

get drunk tonight," Kain grumbled, turning on his heel and stomping towards his office.

I thought about protesting, I didn't want a bachelor party. I wanted to go home to Abby, but Kain looked like he needed some brotherly support. I also couldn't wait to hear his story, after the shit he'd given me about Abby.

"Let me see if I got this right," I slurred after half a dozen whiskeys and forcing the story out of Kain. "You found your mate in San Diego, after you went there to tell my mate what a pathetic loser I was without her, and then you lost your mate, without even learning her last name?"

"Fuck off, dude," Kain grumbled, signaling the waitress for more liquor. "I didn't know she was going to fucking vanish while I was sleeping."

I slapped the table, bent over laughing. "That's why you ran out of the hotel the next morning like your ass was on fire!"

"I thought I might know where to find her, but it was a dead end." He took a big gulp of whiskey, set the empty cup aside and picked up a fresh glass.

Unfortunately, I was keeping pace with him, and was going to be in trouble when I got home. When I texted Abby to tell her that I was going out with Kain, she told me to have fun and said she was going to her apartment for the night. I had every intention of joining her there when I was done here. I had no intention of spending the night without my wife. *Wife.*

"I'm fucking married," I blurted out suddenly. "Abby is my wife!"

"Yeah, congrats by the way." He gave me a little toast with his glass. "I really am happy for you. I know I'm shitty company tonight. We can go to the titty bar and I'll pay for a lap dance, if you want."

"Fuck no!" I barked. "Only woman I want naked on my lap is Abby."

"Figured you'd say that," he grumbled. "That's why we're here, pathetically drinking like a couple of old men."

I downed my whiskey and motioned for more. "Guess we better do it right then."

I lost count of how much we drank, but it was way too much, even for our high metabolism, and we were both drunk as shit. Kain got in his car, letting his driver take him home, but I stupidly decided it was close enough to Abby's apartment to walk since the weather was so nice.

After only a few blocks, my vision was blurry, and I'd somehow managed to get turned around. I knew I was close, but I couldn't find Abby's apartment for the life of me.

"Are you lost, big guy?" A blond guy walked out from somewhere and looked at me curiously.

"Not me. I know this town like the back of my dick." I stumbled and ended up sitting on the curb.

"Uh huh," the guy said. "Where are you trying to go?"

"Abby's apartment is here somewhere." I looked around stupidly.

"All right, put your thumb here." He held a phone in front of me, it looked suspiciously like my phone, but I didn't question it as he pressed my thumb to the screen.

I let my drunken stupor appreciate just how ugly Abby's neighborhood was, and I only caught a few words of what the guy was saying behind me.

"Found a big guy... Drunk off his ass... Lost... Corner of Welsh and Fourth... Need help."

My vision went black, and I might've lain down for a minute. Pretty soon, I felt myself being pushed to my feet.

There was a lot of pushing and pulling. I grumbled the whole time.

"Let me sleep. Leave me alone. Kain, I'm going to kill your dumbass for this."

Someone started pushing my ass as I was crawling up a staircase.

"Don't touch my ass, motherfucker!" I catapulted myself forward, away from the frisky hands, and someone started giggling.

The giggling lit my body up like a match, and to my horror, I was rock hard instantly. That was only for Abby!

After more pushing and pulling, I felt a soft surface under my back, and I knew my cock was making a serious tent in my pants.

"Don't look at my dick, fucker. That's Abby's!"

I'd started to drift into oblivion when hands started working on my pants, and I fought whoever it was off. "Don't touch me! I'll fucking shift and kill you, motherfucker. That's only for Abby! I may be drunk, but Kit would rip your fucking head off! Go away! Leave me alone!"

For some reason I couldn't wrap my head around, Kit was calm and content inside me, not at all concerned about whoever was touching me.

After the hands stopped touching me, I let the alcohol take me under.

A few minutes earlier

Abby

. . .

The second night home and Kade went out with his brother. Not that I minded. I decided to go back to my apartment and work on packing up my stuff since I assumed Kade would want me spending more time at his apartment.

It was boring though, and I was really tired after the last several nights getting thoroughly fucked by my new husband, so I decided to go to bed early. It was weird, the bed was too cold, too big, too empty without Kade beside me.

Luckily, I wasn't dead to the world when the phone rang. I saw Kade's number and answered immediately, thinking he was just telling me that he was here and to come let him in. I got out of bed as I answered, but it wasn't Kade's voice that greeted me, and I felt immediately nauseated and suspicious.

"Is this Abby?" the man said.

"Yes, who the hell is this?" I demanded.

"My name is Ezra. I found a big guy on the street drunk off his ass, he said he was trying to get to Abby's apartment. He's lost but won't admit it." He chuckled through the whole thing, and I breathed a sigh of relief.

I'd seen too many movies where someone uses the man's phone to report cheating. I was still way too insecure.

"Where are you?" I asked calmly

"On the corner of Welsh and Fourth," Ezra said.

"My apartment is right around the corner." I pulled on pants and a sweater.

"Yeah, I'm going to need help getting his large body off the sidewalk," Ezra informed me.

"I'll be right there."

I hung up and ran out of my apartment. I found Kade lying on the sidewalk with a good-looking blond guy staring down at him. He immediately turned as I approached.

"Abby?"

I nodded.

"Lucky I was working late tonight and happened upon

him. He could've been robbed or worse in this neighborhood," Ezra said as we shook hands.

"Yeah, thanks," I muttered lamely. "If I pay you, will you help me get him upstairs?"

"Girl, you don't have to pay me," he scoffed. "What do you think I'm standing out here waiting for you for?"

"The view?" I gestured down at Kade.

"I bet he's pretty hot when he's sober and vertical," Ezra joked. "Kudos to you, but I'm no homewrecker."

After some pulling, we got Kade off the sidewalk and into the building. Ezra and I were mostly silent, with only a few grunts and groans. Kade muttered the whole time, strange, slurred variations of 'leave me alone, let me sleep, and I'm going to kill Kain's dumbass'.

Ezra pulled, I pushed until we reached the stairs, when Kade went face-first, almost crushing Ezra. Kade didn't seem to notice, though, and started crawling up the stairs. I pushed on his butt for momentum, but that only angered him.

"Don't touch my ass, motherfucker!" he bellowed as he launched himself up the stairs and ended up sprawled out on the landing.

I couldn't contain the giggles that burst forth, both at the sight of Kade spread out like a starfish and the look on Ezra's face as he jumped out of the way.

Ezra chuckled, and we both took an arm and lifted Kade to a sitting position. We managed to get him into my apartment, but gave up and let him fall onto the couch. We both stood, panting for breath, while we looked down at his large drunken form.

"Don't look at my dick, fucker. That's Abby's!" Kade roared suddenly.

I covered my mouth to stifle the giggles, and Ezra backed away, his shoulders shaking with silent laughter.

"I'll leave you to it," Ezra said with a wave. "Good luck."

"Thank you so much!" I quickly grabbed a business card and handed it to him. "Text me, and I'll buy you a cup of coffee sometime or something to say thank you properly. I want to hear the whole story."

"You're Abby Bradley?" he gasped. "Girl, I definitely will text you."

I closed and locked the door as he left, figuring I'd let him explain that to me when we had coffee. I turned back to my drunken husband. He didn't look very comfortable. I removed his shoes, but when I started to undo his pants, he freaked out and slapped my hands away.

"Don't touch me!" he yelled belligerently, "I'll fucking shift and kill you, motherfucker. That's only for Abby! I may be drunk, but Kit would rip your fucking head off! Go away! Leave me alone!"

I backed away, covered him with a light blanket, and went to bed. I giggled as I crawled into bed. I knew he didn't know it was me and probably didn't understand his erection, but I didn't feel bad for him.

He was drunk out of his mind, and had fought me off so I wouldn't go near his dick. I have no doubt that if Ezra, or anyone else had tried, he would've shifted and torn the place apart.

I was feeling so much better about everything, finally appreciating what Kade had told me about him not being the kind of man who cheated. Sure, his bear wouldn't allow him to, but the man could still be okay with it. After tonight, it was obvious Kade wasn't.

I smiled and let myself replay every interaction we'd had since the disastrous beginning. Kade was sweet, attentive, loving. It was obvious he was obsessed with me, and even though he was afraid of the power I had, he loved me anyway.

Kade had practically dragged me to the chapel in Las Vegas, but as soon as we'd arrived, he stopped abruptly, grabbed both of my arms and looked at me with a wild desperation.

"Abby, you don't have to do this," he'd said. "I love you, and I'll be happy to just be with you. I don't want you to do this if you're not ready."

At first, I thought he was having cold feet and giving himself an out by turning it on me. I frowned deeply.

"You don't want to..." I began, but he cut me off.

"I do! Of course, I do! I asked you. I just don't want you to regret it." He swallowed thickly and looked away. "Or hate me."

My heart swelled, and I started to understand his concern. He continued before I could voice my opinion.

"I love you, Abby. I'm absolutely crazy about you, and I wouldn't be able to handle it if you hated me or resented me for forcing you into a life you don't want."

"Kade, stop." I put both hands on his chest and gazed up into his glowing eyes. "I should've said this back in San Diego. I love you. I want to marry you. You're my mate, and I know you'll make me happy. We're going to have a baby together. We can move into Greenhope in a few months. One day, you'll give me the daughter I've always wanted. And I promise I'll be faithful and do everything I can to make you happy too."

He'd kissed me with such wild abandon, strangers actually started cheering. I didn't cry when the Elvis-impersonator said you may kiss the bride, but I laughed and launched myself into Kade's strong arms.

The bed was still too empty without Kade next to me, but I could hear him snoring on the couch, and I finally slipped into a peaceful sleep.

September 26th

Abby

. . .

"Kain, I'm going to kill you, you soulless motherfucker." I was awoken by Kade's loud profanity coming from my living room.

I stifled a giggle as I slipped on my robe to see what was going on. Kade was lying on the floor, spread eagle and bare chested. His phone was still on the kitchen table, so he must've been yelling to himself.

"Good morning," I sing-songed, not feeling sorry for his hangover in the slightest. "Coffee?"

"Can you inject it into my veins, baby?" he groaned. "I don't think it'll survive my stomach."

"Poor, Kade," I teased as I started making coffee, more loudly than was really necessary.

"You're mean," he sulked. "You're supposed to feel sorry for me."

"That's strange," I chuckled. "I don't."

"How did I get here?" he asked.

"It was a joint effort," I supplied vaguely.

"Did I fuck you?"

I peeked into the living room and watched him crawl up onto the couch with a frown creasing his handsome face.

"It was a very memorable night," I joked.

"Don't say I fucked you," he groaned.

I stomped into the living room with two cups of coffee, set them down on the coffee table and put my hands on my hips. "What's that supposed to mean?"

"I don't remember!" he wailed helplessly, and I fought the grin threatening to give me away. "I'd hate it if I fucked you and couldn't remember."

"You didn't fuck me." I gave up the charade, feeling a little bit bad after that. "You freaked out when I tried to take your pants off."

He paused halfway while reaching for his coffee and gave

me a smirk. "Were you trying to take advantage, Mrs. Barrett?"

"Mrs. Barrett!" I shrieked suddenly. "I'm Mrs. Barrett!"

"Yeah," he said slowly. "Did you forget already? Vegas? The wedding?"

"No!" I scoffed and threw my hands up. "I knew we'd gotten married, I just didn't realize it meant I was Mrs. Barrett."

Kade rubbed his hands over his face with frustration. "Okay, but we got married. You know that means you're my wife, right?"

I chuckled and plopped myself on the couch next to him. "Oh, Kade, shut up. Of course I do. I just meant, I'd forgotten about the name change thing. I'll have to go to the DMV and the social security administration for new identification."

He relaxed next to me, and we both reached for our coffees.

"I feel like shit," he said after we'd both taken our first drinks. "I have weird ass memories about last night. Some guy and I might've been lost."

"Is that all you remember?" I hedged.

"There might've been something else," he admitted sheepishly.

I sipped my coffee, thoroughly enjoying watching him squirm.

"Something happened, I don't know what exactly," he paused and took a slow drink of coffee while he considered how to tell me. He set the cup down abruptly, and turned to me. "I got a hard-on."

"I know," I tried to ease his worries but he barreled on.

"I don't understand why it happened. Kit was calm inside me. It shouldn't be possible, unless..."

"Unless I was there," I finished for him as his eyes lit up with understanding. "I was the one pushing your ass up the stairs. I was the one trying to wrestle your pants off. I was the 'motherfucker' that you threatened to unleash Kit on."

Kade started laughing, and I set my coffee down quickly before he spilled it. I crawled onto his lap as he hugged me.

"I should've realized," he breathed out a sigh of relief.

"It was pretty damn funny when you were yelling that your dick was only for me," I said.

"Why didn't you say anything?" He nipped at my neck, sending me into a flurry of lust.

"Because it was very educational," I explained as he kissed along my collarbone. "Aren't you hungover?"

"Yes, what does that have to do with anything?" He pulled open my robe and kissed along my cleavage. "My sexy wife climbs onto my lap and everything else is irrelevant."

My phone beeped, and Kade dropped his face into my cleavage with a sigh.

I held it so we both could see the text.

"Who is Ezra and why are you having coffee with him?" Kade demanded on a growl.

"He's the guy that found you last night and helped me drag your giant ass up here," I explained as I typed out a quick response and threw the phone aside. "He was very appreciative of your devilish good looks, but I invited him for coffee to thank him anyway."

"Ah," Kade nodded in understanding. "Fine, but if your assumption turns out wrong and he even looks at you funny, I'll kill him."

"Enough jealousy. Take me to bed, husband." I wrapped my arms and legs around him as he stood and did exactly that.

Chapter 15

September 27th
Abby

I met Ezra the next day for coffee. I told Kade exactly where we'd be just in case he felt like coming to check the guy out. A little part of me hoped he trusted me enough not to, but a big part of me hoped he did since his overprotective nature turned me on.

Ezra agreed to meet me at a little Cafe in downtown Ridgewood. I was anxious to get to West Ridge and check on the progress of my house, but I felt like I owed him.

"Abby Bradley!" he gushed loudly as soon as I walked in, causing a few heads to turn in our direction.

"It's actually Abby Barrett now." I proudly flashed my gorgeous wedding rings as I took the chair across from him.

"Oh, honey, good for you. Tell me that large hunk of man meat is Mr. Barrett." His eyes were bright with humor, but I still stiffened.

"I broke up with my ex-boyfriend after I found him fucking my gay best friend," I blurted. "Please don't call my husband *man meat."*

Ezra just laughed. "Girl, you've got nothing to worry about from me. I might be open and flamboyant with you, but I'd never hit on your man. And besides, bears don't do that shit."

"Shh!" I glanced around the Cafe to see if we had any eavesdroppers.

"This is why we need to meet in West Ridge," he scolded. "We can say the word *bear* without worrying about stray ears."

"I'm working on a house in West Ridge right now, actually. If we meet again, that would be more convenient for me."

A young woman appeared and introduced herself as our waitress, Brittany, and took our orders.

"I live in West Ridge," Ezra said once the waitress was gone. "I was in Ridgewood the other night because the homeowner of a job I'd done had an emergency. Her son had a party and moved some of her furniture and she just couldn't get it back the way it was supposed to be." He said it so dramatically, I smiled.

"How horrible," I tried for flat sarcasm.

"I know it, but I'm flexible," he winked with the innuendo, "and I like to keep my clients happy."

"What do you do, exactly?" I asked as Brittany set our coffees and muffins down. I took a sip of my one coffee of the day and sighed.

"Interior design," he said proudly. "I specialize in the bear designs you see in West Ridge, but I'll also do other stuff in Ridgewood. Gotta pay the bills, you know?"

"Bear designs?" I questioned, nibbling on my muffin.

"Oh, girl, you haven't noticed yet?" He gave me an incredulous look. "Everything is bears in West Ridge. It's all about finding a way to incorporate bears in the decor in a stylish and unique way."

"I mean, I saw the bears at the Bear Cave Cafe, but I figured they were just playing up the name," I admitted.

"Lord, no." He smiled mischievously as he sipped his coffee. "There are bears on the curtains, bears in the artwork, bear knick-knacks and bear lamps."

I grimaced, that could get gaudy.

"I know what you're thinking. Exactly why I use a subtle and clever approach." He took a drink of coffee and looked away, but I saw the playful excitement on his face easily.

"What do you mean?" I pushed.

"Oh, no, girl." He smiled broadly. "You don't get my trade secrets with one cup of coffee. After you agree to let me work with you, we'll become BFFs, and then you can pick my brain."

I laughed at his gall. "I see how you are."

We ate in comfortable silence for a minute.

"I don't really understand why you want to work with me," I confessed. "I renovate old houses."

"Hmm, yes." Ezra nodded. "But, you're the best. You can take a rundown piece of condemned shit and turn it into a contemporary modern home better than anyone. But... can you turn it into a rugged bear cave?"

"I'll tell you what, you show me one of your houses, and I'll show you one of mine." I leaned back and smiled smugly. "And then we can decide if we can handle collaborating on a project."

"Show me yours, I'll show you mine?" he teased. "You saucy minx. I love it. I'm free today."

"Abby?"

As soon as I heard the voice, I groaned. Sending Ezra an apologetic look, I turned to give Simon my best look of disinterest.

"I'm having a very enjoyable breakfast, please don't ruin it," I ground out between clenched teeth.

Ezra's eyes widened with intrigue as Simon's face morphed into disapproval.

"This is exactly what I'm always talking about, Abby." He had the balls to reprimand me. "Why can't you just be nice?"

I opened my mouth to give him a sarcastic retort at the same time I felt my mate's presence. I snapped my mouth shut and just smirked at Simon. He looked at me curiously, and then he had a large hand wrapped around his throat as he was lifted a foot off the ground.

Ezra gasped appropriately. I stood with a dramatic sigh, and Liam shuffled forward reluctantly from where he must've been hiding from me.

"I told you to stay away from her," Kade growled.

"Simon, I don't know if you remember my husband." I placed a hand on Kade's back to help calm him so he didn't actually kill anyone.

Simon could only nod weakly as his face started turning red.

"Put him down!" Liam shrieked suddenly. "He can't breathe."

"Stay out of it," Ezra said and stood suddenly, placing himself between Liam and us.

"Abby!" Liam whined.

I feigned an innocent expression and watched his face morph with anger.

"I can't imagine why he prefers me to you," Liam sneered.

Ezra slapped him across the face suddenly, startling us all.

"I've always wanted to do that," Ezra said, giving me a sheepish smile.

I laughed. "I never would've guessed you weren't an experienced slapper. Oh, Kade, put him down already. He's purple."

Kade dropped Simon suddenly. Simon almost collapsed, but Liam stepped forward and caught him around the waist.

I put my hand on Kade's chest in an obvious display of my wedding rings and spoke slowly and deliberately to Simon and Liam, "This is my overprotective husband." I pointed to my round belly. "This is my husband's baby. We hope to never see you again, but if we do, it would be smart to keep your distance from us in the future."

Simon was still breathing heavily, holding his neck. Liam nodded and dragged Simon away.

"Girl, I love you," Ezra announced once they were gone. "I never see drama like this. That was the most fun I've had in forever."

Kade growled, obviously still on edge.

"Kade, honey," I smiled up at him cheerfully. "You remember Ezra, right? He's my new BFF."

Ezra giggled, and Kade looked between us curiously.

"It's a girl thing," Ezra explained, offering Kade his hand. "Very pleased to meet you officially, Mr. Abby Bradley."

I chuckled at the startled expression on Kade's face. He looked down at me, but I just shrugged. Kade shook Ezra's hand roughly.

"You're just in time to pay for coffee, big daddy," I teased, feeling light-hearted and playful.

Ezra bit his lip to hide the grin. Kade threw a few twenties on the table, way too much for the bill, but probably as a silent apology for the scene we'd made, and led me out of the cafe by the elbow. As soon as we were outside, he pulled me into him and kissed me possessively.

We broke apart, both gasping for breath, and saw Ezra fanning himself jokingly a few feet away.

"You two make fire look subarctic," he quipped.

"How do you make him go away?" Kade grumbled.

"I don't know yet." I shrugged. "But we have houses to see, so we'll have to finish this later."

"But..." Kade protested, rubbing his groin against me, almost making me lose all rational thought.

"Down boy!" Ezra yelled. "Two hours, three tops. Then she can meet you at home and fuck you into next week."

"Don't make promises like that for me!" I insisted. "He'd take it literally and try to keep me in bed until next week."

Ezra snickered, and Kade rolled his eyes.

"You two are too much," Kade kissed my forehead. "I'm going back to work then if you don't need me."

Kade glared at Ezra. "If you look at either one of us wrong, it'll be the last thing you ever do."

"Threat received, and dutifully followed." Ezra gave him a mock salute. "I will never give you a reason to think I'm anything less than friendly towards either of you." Ezra gave him a cheeky smile and then added, "Sound good, big daddy?"

I wrapped my arms around Kade to stop him from lunging at Ezra and laughed against his chest.

Kade looked down at me with adoration and kissed my forehead, mumbling, "Only because he makes you laugh. See you soon, baby."

Kade

It had been four hours since the episode at the Cafe and I paced my apartment anxiously waiting for her to get home.

I hadn't meant to go to the Cafe this morning, wanting to prove I trusted her, but, well, she sent me the address and it was so close to my office. It was almost like she wanted me to. It was easy to just pop out for a coffee and say hello.

Until I saw her ex standing by the table and lost my shit.

I'd wanted to pop his head like the zit he was. Her reassuring touch was the only thing that grounded me.

Even I'd admit that her friend slapping the other guy had been pretty damn funny, but I forgot to confirm it was Liam. I'd pretty much decided to like Ezra after that, but I still needed to give him a firm warning.

I'd almost lost it when he called me big daddy, that was for Abby, even if it was pretty damn amusing too. The guy had a pair on him, I'd give him that. As long as he made Abby laugh and didn't try anything, he was fine with me.

"Kade!" Abby squealed as she entered, startling me.

I'd been so lost in my thoughts, I'd forgotten I was waiting for her so I could fuck her until she couldn't walk. I was still a little amped up from earlier.

"Look at these!" Abby held up two little wood carved bears. One was wearing a suit and the other one had a bow on its head. "They're salt and pepper shakers!"

I smiled at her adorable delight. "Okay."

"They're darling," she huffed at my obvious lack of taste. "Ezra took me to this little store, Bare Home Furnishings, and showed me all these wood carvings by this guy, G.R. Black. Apparently every home in West Ridge wants some."

"And now ours will have some?" I asked as I stalked towards her slowly.

She was too busy with her find, she didn't notice until my arms were firmly wrapped around her, and my erection grinding against her ass.

"You're insatiable," she sighed, setting her treasure aside.

"Excuse me? It's been like twelve hours since I've been inside you." I nipped at her neck and licked my mark.

"Can we not have one conversation like adults?" she asked, but her tone was amused and she wrapped her arms around me.

"Sure." I kissed her lips, cutting off any words she might have to say.

After I'd released some of my pent-up frustration, twice, and given her several orgasms, we lay together on the bed, completely sated.

"What did you want to talk about, then?" I asked.

She laughed. "Ezra, Kain, our house, our apartments, our marriage, our baby, our lives. You know, adult stuff."

"Oh fine," I huffed teasingly. "If we have to."

"We can't just have sex every moment of every day for the rest of our lives," she scolded.

"I know that," I scoffed. "But there's fucking, and making love, and blow jobs."

She smacked my chest and started to get out of bed. I grabbed her and pulled her into my chest.

"I'm teasing, wife," I assured her as I kissed her cheek. "Don't go. I like you right here. I'll talk about whatever you want. I'll tell you all about Kain and how he lost his mate in San Diego. You can tell me all about your weird little friend and your bear shakers. Then we'll agree on where we live until you're done with the house."

"That sounds good, except I want to go first." She smiled sweetly.

"The floor is yours."

We cuddled and talked until her belly rumbled, and then we ate supper and talked some more. I was just as content talking with her as I was doing everything else with her.

When we ran out of words, I made love to her and we fell asleep wrapped in each other's arms.

It was utterly perfect. I could definitely handle being with her for the next fifty years and for the first time, I wasn't even scared.

Epilogue

January 18th
Kade

"I fucking hate you, Kade Barrett!" she screamed miserably. "I'm going to chop your fucking dick off if you ever think about doing this to me again!"

I let her squeeze the life out of my hand and brushed her hair back off her forehead.

"You're doing great, baby," I whispered soothingly. "You're amazing."

"Fuck you! Don't be sweet to me while I'm yelling at you!" she raved.

"All right, Abby, another push," the doctor instructed.

Abby pushed with all her might as she cussed me out. "You're never fucking me again! Do you hear me? Never! You big fucking asshole!"

The sound of our baby boy's cry stopped her instantly, and she whooshed out a gust of air.

"Congratulations, Mommy," the nurse said as she laid the beautiful bundle in Abby's outstretched arms.

"He's perfect," Abby whispered, a tear rolling down her cheek.

"He's beautiful," I agreed, kissing her forehead. "Just like you."

She may have just screamed all of my worst fears at me, but I knew she didn't mean them. Abby loved me, and she showed me every day. I knew that she knew I loved her too. I was obsessed with her and couldn't help showering her with love and affection.

Abby tipped her head up to me, and I gave her a chaste kiss.

"Sorry about all that," she said sheepishly. "I didn't mean most of it."

"I know, we still have to have your daughter, at least," I reminded her.

"Um, no, I was serious about that part." She scowled at me. "I will chop it off."

I covered my groin defensively. I figured I'd give her a year or so to forget this conversation before I tried again.

I took our new bundle from Abby and cradled him to my chest. I had a son. It was a humbling feeling, but I'd never felt more like a man.

"Do you have a name picked out?" the doctor asked.

"Kadence Diego Barrett," Abby told her wistfully.

She beamed up at me, and I couldn't stop myself from kissing her again. My wife. My family. How did I ever get so lucky?

"I love you, Kade," Abby said as I returned our son to her tender embrace.

"I love you too, Abby." I kissed her forehead. "Kain and his mate are in the waiting room when you're ready for visitors."

Abby sighed as the baby latched onto her breast and suckled greedily. I had some very inappropriate comments about that, but managed to keep them to myself since the nurse and doctor were still milling about.

She nodded and smiled serenely. My heart was practically ready to burst in my chest.

January 22nd

Abby

We laid Kadence in his gorgeously crafted bassinet and gazed down at him in awe. He's such a little miracle. Utterly perfect, and already has both Kade and me wrapped around his little finger.

I can barely believe we've come so far. Just last year, I was alone and pathetic, wallowing in self-pity after my breakup with Simon.

Now I have a husband who thinks I'm perfect, which I'll never admit to not being, and a baby boy who couldn't be more perfect if he tried. He already looks so much like Kade, I just know he's going to be a lady killer.

I'll make sure he grows up with a positive attitude towards women and mates though, hopefully save him – and his mate – from some of the drama we went through.

"You need to sleep, too," Kade whispered in my ear as he wrapped his arms around me, gently pulling me away.

I knew I'd told him I'd cut his dick off if he tried to impregnate me again, but…

"I think we should wait nine months," I informed Kade as

he closed the door to the nursery with a soft click. "Then our kids will be eighteen months apart."

He looked at me with amusement.

"Yes, I know what I said," I huffed before he could call me out on it. "But I do want a daughter."

"What if we have another boy?" he asked.

"Then I'll cut it off," I threatened, and he chuckled. "I'd like two kids. Maybe three. Four tops."

He laughed at my indecisiveness.

"Being an only child sucks," I explained.

"Baby, you know I'll give you whatever you want." He wrapped me in his arms, and I laid my head on his chest.

"Hmm," I purred. "And that's one of the many things I love about you."

K. C. Woods

You know when you get a song stuck in your head for days and days? That's what it's like for me when I get an idea for a new story. It replays in my head, over and over, each time expanding a little further (characters, plot, setting, background, dialogue), until I'm forced to sit down and purge it onto paper. It started when I was in my late teens and, with any luck, will continue into senility.

My name is K.C. Woods. I was born and raised in Small Town, Minnesota. I work full-time as a travel nurse. I'm blessed with a supportive husband and four sassy daughters. The majority of my time is spent working, writing, and spending time with my family. I also do a lot of reading (always romance, but sub-genres vary with my mood).

Don't miss these exciting titles by K. C. Woods and Blushing Books!

West Ridge Bears

Kade's Mate – Book One

Blushing Books

Blushing Books is the oldest eBook publisher on the web. We've been running websites that publish steamy romance and erotica since 1999, and we have been selling eBooks since 2003. We have free and promotional offerings that change weekly, so please do visit us at http://www.blushingbooks.com/free.

Blushing Books Newsletter

Please join the Blushing Books newsletter
to receive updates & special promotional offers.
You can also join by using your mobile phone:
Just text BLUSHING to 22828.

Every month, one new sign up via text messaging will receive
a $25.00 Amazon gift card, so sign up today!

www.ingramcontent.com/pod-product-compliance
Lightning Source LLC
LaVergne TN
LVHW090951080826
845145LV00003B/966

* 9 7 8 1 6 4 5 6 3 6 4 1 0 *